KU-792-563

With two beautiful daughters, **Lucy Ryder** has had to curb her adventurous spirit and settle down. But because she's easily bored by routine she's turned to writing as a creative outlet and to romances because—'What else is there other than chocolate?' Characterised by friends and family as a romantic cynic, Lucy can't write serious stuff to save her life. She loves creating characters who are funny, romantic and just a little cynical.

Also by Lucy Ryder

Resisting Her Rebel Hero
Tamed by Her Army Doc's Touch
Falling at the Surgeon's Feet
Caught in a Storm of Passion

Rebels of Port St John's miniseries

Rebel Doc on Her Doorstep
Resisting Her Commander Hero

Discover more at millsandboon.co.uk.

PREGNANT BY THE PLAYBOY SURGEON

LUCY RYDER

MILLS & BOON

All rights reserved including the right of reproduction
in whole or in part in any form. This edition is
published by arrangement with Harlequin Books S.A.

This is a work of fiction. Names, characters,
places, locations and incidents are purely fictional
and bear no relationship to any real life individuals,
living or dead, or to any actual places, business
establishments, locations, events or incidents.
Any resemblance is entirely coincidental.

This book is sold subject to the condition that it
shall not, by way of trade or otherwise, be lent, resold,
hired out or otherwise circulated without the prior consent
of the publisher in any form of binding or cover
other than that in which it is published and without a
similar condition including this condition being
imposed on the subsequent purchaser.

® and TM are trademarks owned and used by the
trademark owner and/or its licensee. Trademarks
marked with ® are registered with the United Kingdom
Patent Office and/or the Office for Harmonisation in the
Internal Market and in other countries.

First published in Great Britain 2019
by Mills & Boon, an imprint of HarperCollins*Publishers*
1 London Bridge Street, London, SE1 9GF

Large Print edition 2019

© 2019 Bev Riley

ISBN: 978-0-263-07851-0

MIX
Paper from
responsible sources
FSC
www.fsc.org   FSC™ C007454

This book is produced from independently certified
FSC™ paper to ensure responsible forest management. For
more information visit www.harpercollins.co.uk/green.

Printed and bound in Great Britain
by CPI Group (UK) Ltd, Croydon, CR0 4YY

To anyone who's ever
faced heartbreak and triumphed,
this one's for you.

CHAPTER ONE

ER PHYSICIAN DR. DANIELLE STEVENS crossed the parking lot toward the employees' entrance of St. Mary's hospital in downtown Vancouver with the sneaky feeling that her life had been cursed. If she didn't know better she would swear it was Friday the thirteenth and the universe was having fun at her expense.

She'd woken to rain—not exactly an unusual occurrence in Vancouver—and then discovered her shower was on the fritz and the water pipes were making alarming noises. Of course that meant she'd have to forgo her showers until she got someone to check it out. If that hadn't been bad enough, she'd been out of coffee because she'd forgotten to stop at the supermarket and stock up on the basics. Basics like coffee, peanut butter, cheese curls and hair conditioner. Which meant not only was she caffeine-deprived, she was also starving and having a hair day from hell.

Then she'd found an unwelcome gift—a half-chewed bird missing its head—courtesy of her neighbor Hilda Frauenbach's cat Axel.

Yuck.

And, because her car was *still* in the workshop, she'd had to hotfoot it ten blocks in the pouring rain.

Good times.

Good times that were bound to continue rolling because although today might not be the thirteenth, it *was* Friday. And Friday nights in the ER could only be described as the second level of hell, because by the end of the work week any good sense people might have decreased in direct proportion to the amount of alcohol they consumed.

Trying to ignore the sneaky feeling that her life was unraveling, Dani felt her hip vibrate and paused to dig her phone out of her shoulder bag.

Thinking it was her mechanic, with yet another lame excuse as to why her car hadn't been fixed, she swiped irritably at the screen only to discover a Facebook notification inviting her to check on what Richard Ashford-Hall the Turd—oops, the Third—was doing in Cabo Mexico.

She took great pleasure in deleting the notification with a decisive jab. "No," she told the screen firmly, ignoring the sick, shaky feeling she usually got when Richard's name was mentioned. "I do *not* want to see what that sick, cheating rat-fink bastard is up to now, thank you very much."

And frankly, she had even less interest in seeing with whom he was doing it. She just hoped the woman knew what she was getting herself into.

She hadn't but that chapter in her life was closed.

Thank God.

She just wished people would stop reminding her of how stupid, naïve and trusting she'd been—or how fabulous her life could have been if she'd been prepared to stay married to a serial liar, a habitual cheater and an all-round spoilt man-brat.

She shivered as memories of her marriage assailed her. She'd rather be living on a houseboat that was falling to pieces with questionable plumbing, eating peanut butter and cheese curls for the rest of eternity than be back in the vipers' pit that was the Ashford-Hall family.

Heck, she'd rather be dealing with Axel's unsuspecting gifts than having to deal with spoilt, entitled rich boys and their creepy friends.

Noticing there was a voice message from the mechanic, Dani accessed it, grimacing when, "Hey, Sweetness!" emerged loudly. She quickly turned down the volume before someone overheard. "Listen, it's about your car. Are you sure you don't want me to contact a friend who can give you a good deal on a trade-in for this wreck? I'm sure we could work out some kind of payment arrangement," he said.

His voice was heavy with insinuation that made her skin crawl—*double yuck*—and reminded her of the men belonging to the super-elite club her ex had belonged to.

"Besides, there's a whole bunch of frayed wires that I'm having a hard time identifying and there's more rust here than an old tug boat. Call me. *Anytime*."

Annoyed, she called the mechanic back and got the workshop's answering machine because the work week had already ended. *Damn.*

"This is Danielle Stevens," she said firmly. "Negative on the trade-in and the intro to your friend."

She was pretty sure the guy had illegal contacts, and she had no intention of acquiring stolen property. She might want to do things as cheaply as possible but buying a hot car wasn't one of them.

"Just fix my car!" she yelled. About to disconnect, she added a better late than never "please," because her mom had taught her that people tended not to respond positively to rudeness.

Drawing in a lungful of air, she held it for a couple of seconds before slowly expelling it along with her irritation.

There. Look at her being all Zen and going with the flow.

Okay, so maybe she wasn't going with the flow so much as dealing. Besides, it wasn't like dealing was anything new. So she was going to be without her car again this weekend? No big deal. It just meant she'd be walking the gazillion blocks to the marina after her shift. She'd done that before and survived too. It had been in her student days but she was still young, right—if thirty could be called young—and she was pretty sure a six-hundred-mile walk was good for her.

Besides, hadn't she noticed just yesterday that her jeans were getting a little tight? This way she could get that much-needed exercise she was always promising herself without having to give up peanut butter or cheese curls.

It would be good for her. Great, even. Unlike the two years she'd spent as Mrs. Ashford-Hall. Two years she could never get back. Two years—make that three—she would give anything to erase from her memory.

Muttering about the questionable heritage of the entire male race—car mechanics, landlords and ex-husbands especially—she stepped out from behind a line of parked cars just as an SUV roared past, hooting at her, the dumb woman not looking where she was going, and drenching her with a lovely mix of dirt, rainwater and God knew what else in the process.

She gave a gasping shriek and lurched backward, arms windmilling frantically as she stumbled over the uneven surface of the road. The next instant she collided with the bumper behind her and went down like a felled cypress.

Knocked from her hand, her phone went one way and her shoulder bag the other, spilling its contents across the asphalt.

Stunned, and spluttering with shock at finding herself sprawled in the road, Dani closed her eyes for a dozen rapid heartbeats, wondering what the hell she'd done to deserve this day. She felt movement in the air around her and opened her eyes to see a pair of concerned moss-green eyes looking down at her from about a foot away.

Whoa. Where did he come from?

Pretty sure she wasn't dead, she blinked up into a face so ruggedly beautiful it might easily have graced the silver screen—or her most private fantasies if she hadn't been taking a kind of permanent hiatus from the entire male race.

Even so... She couldn't prevent her fascinated gaze from taking in a high, broad forehead surrounded by thick dark glossy hair, high cheekbones, strong nose, square jaw and a firm, masculine mouth perfectly framed by a couple-hours-past-five-o'clock shadow.

The stubble gave his square jaw a toughness that suggested he was Alpha to the bone and didn't care who knew it. For a split second she had an overwhelming urge to reach out and trace his sculpted mouth, maybe feel that rough, obvious sign of masculinity...but that would just be the shock talking.

Her fingers tingled, as though she'd given in to the impulse to touch his jaw, and it took another couple of beats to realize he was talking.

"You okay?"

The rough tones slid across her senses like a

mini-orgasm and she froze as unwelcome tingles spread to places deep inside her that had been dead for three long years. She looked down, expecting to see her clothes melted right off her body or maybe steam rising from the soaked fabric because he was hotness personified.

Panic immediately gripped her throat at the realization.

Oh, no, she instructed herself firmly. *Absolutely no tingling for anything with a Y-chromosome. You're done with the whole male race, remember?*

Done. Finished. *Finito.*

"Ma'am, did you hit your head?"

Ma'am? Seriously? Since when was she a "ma'am" to a hot guy? She wasn't *that* old and, looking at the fine laugh lines at the corners of his eyes, she was pretty sure she was a good bit younger than he was.

Realizing that she was staring up at him like an idiot, she opened her mouth to say *I'm fine*, because that was her mantra, and was mortified when a rasp emerged instead. It looked as if her breath had been knocked out along with her remaining brain cells.

Desperate to regain her dignity, she shoved dripping hair out of her eyes and sat up, biting her lip to prevent a moan from emerging when pain radiated out from her hip and elbow.

Before she could stand, he dropped a large warm hand on her shoulder—probably to stop her from throwing herself at him, because she could totally see that happening to him.

With other women, she amended hastily. *Not her.* Nope, she was made of much sterner stuff and she'd given up on his species.

"Stay there a moment," he ordered but he needn't have bothered.

She'd spent her entire marriage being ordered around and she was done taking orders from anyone not responsible for her salary. Besides, she was sitting in a cold puddle of rainwater that was soaking into her jeans and sweater, finding its way into some pretty uncomfortable places.

"Um…" Great—now she was speechless. "I don't think so," she muttered, scrambling to her feet and wincing as a host of places hurt. Chief among them her pride.

It was then she realized that he was holding her shoulder bag in one large tanned hand and gathering up its scattered contents. He should have looked ridiculous but the feminine accessory just made him appear more masculine, if that was possible.

Balanced effortlessly on the balls of his feet, he reached for an unopened box of tampons and had her groaning in embarrassment—although she had no idea why. She was a doctor, for heaven's sake, and it wasn't as if it had burst open, scattering tampons all over Vancouver.

Sunglasses followed, and when he picked up the latest Janet Evanovich novel that she'd bought a couple days ago instead of groceries, he paused, turning to the back so he could read the blurb.

She tried to grab it but he held it out of reach until he'd finished. "Two hot guys?" he queried curiously, as though *she* was the crazy fictional character hooked on a hot cop and an even hotter bounty hunter.

Rolling her eyes, she grabbed the book, her bag and began stuffing everything inside. What she didn't see was her phone or her wallet, which made her panic because it held her last twenty dollars in change. Dani glanced around to find her rescuer holding the battered leather wallet and checking out her hospital ID badge—the one with the picture where she looked like a complete psycho—tilting his head as he studied the photo.

He looked amused, damn him.

With a sound that resembled a panicked squawk, she snatched it from him and stuffed it into the depths of her bag, ignoring the grin and the one arched brow that filled her with irritated envy because she'd have *killed* to have had that talent during her marriage. A talent that conveyed a whole host of emotions from disbelief and skepticism to outright condescension.

His was filled with a masculine amusement that threatened to derail her thought processes.

Out of the corner of her eye she finally spied her phone, and had to get down on all fours and really stretch to retrieve it from under a nearby car. With it finally in her hand she turned—in time to catch him staring at her backside.

She must have made a sound of protest—okay, more of a protesting squawk—because his teeth flashed as his green gaze slowly rose up the front of her dirty, soaked sweater to linger on her mouth before lifting to her eyes.

And, wow. Look at that, she thought with horror as her nipples tightened into painful little points of arousal. Seemed her body wasn't dead after all.

"I'm taking a break from anything with a Y-chromosome," she blurted out, and wanted to crawl back under the car when his low chuckle slid across her senses like rough velvet, sending goose bumps skittering across her skin.

Heat rose up her neck into her cheeks and she gave in to the urge to cover her face in the guise of shoving her hair off her face. *Oh God.* What the heck was wrong with her mouth today?

"Good to know," he drawled. "Though it does explain the expiration date."

Huh? Peeking through her fingers, she found him holding up a square foil package that looked suspiciously like…*a condom*? Her eyes widened and she backed away from it as though it might bite.

"Um… I…uh," she stuttered, looking around frantically for an escape route while fighting a hysterical laugh—because she hadn't needed one of those in so long she probably wouldn't know what to do with it. "That's not…" She shook her head desperately and backed away. "Nope. *Definitely* not m-mine."

She scrubbed both hands down her face and

moaned in embarrassment when he bent his knees to peer straight into her eyes. *God. He was even hotter up close.*

"You sure you're okay? You took a pretty hard fall."

She was absolutely *not* going to discuss her graceless tumble, her sore bottom or anything else. "I'm fine, really," she said quickly, desperately wishing it was true, desperately wishing she could just disappear. Because it was bad enough that anyone had witnessed the embarrassing incident. That it was the hottest guy in the Northern hemisphere just proved her theory that the universe was out to get her.

"What about this?" he asked, holding up the unopened condom.

She nearly choked. "I...um...you keep it," she finished in a breathless rush.

"Thanks," he said wryly. "But what if *you* need it?"

She pressed her lips together and shook her head frantically. "I won't," she assured him hurriedly. "I'm taking a break, remember?"

His mouth curled in a half-grin that was filled with wicked trouble as he reached out to tuck a wet curl behind her ear. "So you said."

The move was so unexpected that she stilled, feeling the rough pads of his fingers brush the sensitive skin of her ear. Unexpected because it sent a bunch of pleasurable sensations skittering across her skin. And unexpected because… because she couldn't remember the last time a man had touched her; the last time she'd actually *wanted* a man to touch her.

And she suddenly did. With frightening need. *Ack!*

That it was happening now with a complete stranger was more than a little unnerving.

She licked her lips and shifted nervously.

"Just out of curiosity…" Hot Guy murmured.

He was clearly oblivious to the melting going on inside her head…and, fine, in her thighs too. Melting that left her dizzy and a little too turned on for comfort.

"Does that mean you're currently into women, then?" He looked intrigued, as if he was picturing her kissing another woman when she'd been picturing kissing him.

"What?" Her mouth dropped open and the dizziness vanished. *"No!"* she practically yelped, knocking his hand aside and backing up a couple of steps. "Not that there's anything wrong with that but no, I am not into… *Sheesh!*" Rolling her eyes, she blew out an exasperated breath. "You are such a…a *guy!*"

"Guilty," he murmured, eyes wicked. "But I'm glad."

"Glad?"

"That Sweet 'n Sassy isn't batting for the other team."

Slapping a hand over her eyes, she blurted out, "Oh, my God!" She wished the ground would open up and swallow her. "Please, *please*, stop talking." She gave a laughing groan and pointed a finger in his direction. "And forget you heard that. In fact, forget the last ten minutes altogether because… Oh, *great*," she muttered, catching sight of a couple of co-workers at the entrance, gesturing at her to hurry up and pointing at their watches. "Gotta go."

She was about to step into the road when she was brought up short against a warm, hard— extremely hard—chest as a car whooshed past. "Careful," he murmured in her ear and for the second time in ten minutes Dani experienced that full-body shiver.

Yeah, Dani, she lectured herself silently as her

knees wobbled. *Great advice.* She'd be wise to heed it.

Fortunately it gave her the impetus she needed to mutter an apology and limp across the road toward the employee entrance. Safely on the other side, she felt inexplicably drawn to look over her shoulder—only to find him watching her retreat, a small baffled smile curving that incredibly sexy mouth. As though he couldn't believe what he'd just experienced.

"Thank you," she called out, ignoring the niggling feeling in her gut that she was walking away from something good. Something exciting and…terrifying.

His mouth curved. "Any time."

She paused again, unsure why she couldn't seem to walk away, because she was pretty sure she should be running.

For long seconds they eyed each other across the wet road, until he finally gave a low laugh and asked in a rough, deep voice that slid into places she hadn't known were lonely, "Are you sure you won't reconsider your embargo?"

Was she?

"Nope," she said firmly, shaking her head with jerky exaggerated movements that should con-

vince him—or was that her? So for good measure she added; "I most definitely will *not*."

Liar. You so would.

He was silent for a long beat, his gaze searching, before finally nodding. "My loss," he said
and dug his keys out of his pocket. "See you
around, sweet thing."

The sentiment that just fifteen minutes ago
had made her want to gag filled her with a warm
pleasure that no doubt came from hitting her
head. Then her brain finally caught up and she
gave herself a mental head-slap.

He hadn't meant anything by that parting shot,
she told herself as she reluctantly turned away.
Men flirted all the time. It was a kind of pas-
time…like drinking beer, burping and cheating.
Besides, she had enough problems without adding a tall, sexy stranger with a kind streak to her
things to obsess about.

The most pressing thing, she decided as she
hobbled up the ramp, being that she was late for
her shift and looked as if she'd been moonlight-
ing as a mud wrestler.

Dylan St. James found himself smiling as he
headed toward his Jeep. There hadn't been a

whole lot to smile about lately but the hot little mess he'd just walked away from had done what no one else had in far too long. She'd taken him out of his head and made him smile—laugh, even—which was a miracle considering everything that had happened in the last two years.

He'd lost his grandfather after a long, protracted battle with esophageal cancer and a friend to a climbing accident—all in the space of two months. Reeling from the double whammy, he'd accepted a temporary commission on a West African Mercy Ship, thinking the change would help him deal.

He'd immersed himself in doing what he loved: helping people—kids especially—get to live relatively normal lives with his skill as an orthopedic reconstruction surgeon. Helping those who usually didn't have access to modern medical care.

He'd met some great people and had fallen into a casual relationship with an on-board co-ordinator—a relationship that had been more about propinquity and convenience than any deeper feelings, on his part at least. It didn't say much for him but he'd thought they were friends with on-again, off-again benefits—right

up until Simone had dropped her bombshell…
she was pregnant.

Yeah. Big shock that, considering that they'd
lately been more off than on and he'd never had
unprotected sex. *Ever.* Still, that hadn't been the
worst of it, because although he'd been willing
to face up to his responsibility—without getting
married to someone he didn't have deep feelings
for—she'd had other ideas.

Ideas that had emerged one night when he'd
finished surgery earlier than expected and headed
over to the mess hall for dinner, inadvertently
overhearing Simone and an Australian nurse discussing him—or rather his family's money. Simone had been bragging that she'd managed to
catch herself a rich Canadian doctor—her sole
reason for working in such God-forsaken countries on a boat that didn't even have a swimming
pool.

As if that was important on a hospital ship.

He'd been about to reveal himself when he'd
heard something even more enlightening—that
the baby she was trying to pass off as his belonged to a Mercy Ship colleague. A *married*
colleague.

To say she'd been shocked when she'd looked

up and seen him standing there was an under-statement. There'd been tears, pleas, threats and hysterics but in the end he had been done. He'd finished his contract and come home.

She wasn't the first woman who'd thrown her-self at him after learning that his family owned the largest shipbuilding company in the Pacific Rim and she probably wouldn't be the last. He'd just have to be more careful, that was all. Be-sides, he wasn't interested in marrying someone he couldn't see himself growing old with.

Not that he was against marriage. He wasn't. But he hadn't found a woman who wanted *him* rather than what his family's money could do for her. Hadn't found a woman with whom he could build the kind of relationship his parents and grandparents had.

He sometimes wondered if he ever would.

Arriving at his Jeep, he keyed open the door and slid inside. About to shove his key into the ignition, he realized he was still holding the con-dom. Tossing it into his console, he chuckled at the horrified embarrassment on the woman's face and her insistence that it wasn't hers.

Now, *there* was a feisty little bundle of con-tradictions, he thought, picturing her huge gray

LUCY RYDER

eyes as she'd blurted out that she was taking a break from anything with a Y-chromosome, stirring up all kinds of mixed emotions he hadn't been ready to feel.

Shaking his head at himself, Dylan cranked up the engine. Reversing out of the parking bay, he drove toward the exit, feeling much more cheerful than when he'd landed a few hours ago. He had a few days to catch up with his family and then he'd be back in the saddle at St. Mary's as a consultant.

And if the thought of seeing a certain hot little doctor again made him smile with anticipation he chalked it up to the long flight, three days without much sleep and eight months of celibacy.

CHAPTER TWO

DYLAN FELL BACK into the hospital routine as if he'd only been gone for a week. His old partner, Steve Randall, had been so delighted to have him back that he'd cleared his calendar and headed for the South Pacific, leaving Dylan to handle any upcoming surgeries that couldn't be postponed.

Although he'd have liked to say he was too busy to think about the sweet little brunette from the parking lot, it was kind of disconcerting to discover that he was as susceptible as the next guy to a pair of soft gray eyes and a sweet sassy smile.

He was thirty-five, for God's sake. A surgeon. He'd been dating for twenty years; having sex for almost that long, and he'd never—not once— thought about a woman during surgery.

That was until he'd looked into the smoky eyes of an irresistible brunette as he'd reached for the scattered contents of her purse.

Not only had she invaded his dreams but the Zen-like calm he usually adopted in the OR as well. It had to stop. Distraction was costly—especially in his profession. With Steve off in Bora Bora he didn't have time to take a lunch break, let alone think about a woman determined to stick to her man embargo.

He wondered what had happened to leave her so wary and mistrustful of men. And if he experienced an inexplicable urge to find the guy who'd done it and pound him into the ground it was only because he had two sisters and would do the same to any guy who messed with them.

Yeah, he assured himself, he was feeling protective in an entirely *fraternal* way. It certainly wasn't because his ego had taken a little beating. Besides, he knew next to nothing about her other than the fact she worked at St. Mary's. Even if he'd wanted to prove to himself that he'd imagined the entire incident, St. Mary's was a large hospital. She could work anywhere, and he didn't have the time—or the inclination, he assured himself—to hunt down a woman who wasn't interested.

It was just as well that she'd turned him down because he wasn't looking for anything more

than the occasional good time with an attractive woman who knew the score. And since she
hadn't seemed like the "occasional" type, or even
a "good-time" girl, he would forget all about her
and focus on cementing his professional reputation.

With back-to-back appointments and two solid
days of surgery, by the Thursday evening of the
following week Dylan was ready to call it a day.
He grabbed his leather jacket and turned off the
lights as he walked through the darkened waiting room. It was after eight and he had plans to
meet up with a couple of kayaking friends at a
sports bar near the marina. He hadn't seen them
since his return and was eager to get back on
the water.

He dug in his pocket for his Jeep keys and was
about to lock the door behind him when his cell
phone rang. A quick glance at the caller ID had
him smiling. "Hi, Mom, what's wrong?"

His mother's light, familiar laugh floated
through the phone. "Nothing's *wrong*, darling.
I'm just calling to find out how my favorite son
is doing on his first week back and to invite him
to dinner."

"Mom, I'm your *only* son."

"Still my favorite," she teased. "But don't tell your sisters."

Dylan chuckled, because he'd heard his mother tell his sisters the same thing. "I'd love dinner, Mom but I'm on call. It'll take too long to get back from West Vancouver if there's an emergency."

"That's the beauty of my plan, darling," said Vivian St. James smugly. "We're having dinner at the Regis with the Hendersons. You remember Fred and Daphne, don't you?"

For some reason his mother's overly bright, chatty tone put Dylan's senses on alert. He grimaced when her next words confirmed his suspicions.

"Well, their daughter Abigail is back from Europe, and we can all have a wonderful dinner tog—"

And there it was. "Mom," he interrupted gently. "Don't."

There was a short pause, then a bewildered, "Don't what, darling?"

Dylan sighed. "You're trying to set me up again."

"Don't be silly!"

His mother gave a laughing snort but Dylan

could tell that he'd hit the nail on the head. His mother was trying to get him a date in the hopes that it would lead to the altar. She wanted grandchildren before she died—which was ridiculous because she wasn't yet sixty.

"Even if that's true, young man," she said in her "mom voice"—the one that said he was being deliberately uncooperative. "And I'm not saying it is, you need to get out and meet people. Women."

"Mom, I meet women every day. Besides, I *have* met someone," he heard himself say.

And then he wanted to slap himself upside the head for giving his mother false hope. Vivian would hound him until she met the mythical woman herself. He loved his mother fiercely but if she thought one of her brood needed a helping nudge in the right direction she wasn't above using both hands.

"You have?"

Oh, hell. His mother sounded so delighted at the prospect that her son was dating again after his friend's death. She thought all her children were amazing and wouldn't be able to resist meddling.

"That's wonderful, darling. Where did you meet and when can I meet her?"

No pressure there, St. James, he thought with amused exasperation. "Who says it's a her?"

There was a moment's stunned silence on the other end of the phone and Dylan could picture his mother's expression.

Then Vivian snorted. "Dylan Thomas St. James!" She chuckled. "There's nothing wrong with being gay but I know you're only trying to wind me up. So, when can I meet her?"

Fortunately he was saved from replying when his phone beeped an incoming call. *Talk about being saved by the beep.*

"Just a sec, Mom. I've got a call coming in." With a flick of his hand he accessed the call. "St. James."

"This is Rona Sheppard from the ER," a brisk voice said. "Are you still in the building?"

"I am," he said, shrugging out of his leather jacket and reaching for his lab coat because any call that included the words *Are you still in the building?* meant he wouldn't be going anywhere for a while. "What's up?"

"A young child with a traumatic arm injury," the supervisor said briskly. "ETA three minutes—vitals shaky."

"I'll be right down," he said before disconnecting, his mind already flying ahead to the case.

He was about to shove his phone in his pocket when he remembered his mother.

"Mom," he said, returning to his call. "I'm sorry but I won't make dinner tonight." He didn't say he'd been headed to Harry's on the marina anyway—mostly to prevent the lecture he knew would follow about the kind of women who hung out in sports bars.

"Oh, darn." Vivian sighed. "I've been giddy with happiness since you got back."

She very obviously *didn't* say she was disappointed that he wouldn't meet their friends' daughter but Dylan could read between the lines.

"Is it something bad?"

"I don't know yet but it's a little kid."

"Oh, darling, I know how much you hate these cases. Call me when you can."

He said goodbye and disconnected, taking the stairs instead of waiting for the elevator, because traumatic injuries were always bad. That it was a child made it that much more urgent.

Dylan had spent enough time in the ER to

appreciate that when children were involved emotions ran high. It was one of the worst parts of working in trauma and he held a huge respect for the people who dealt with it on a daily basis.

Even as he hit the swing doors and headed down the hallway he could hear someone rapping out orders in a soft, feminine voice that sent skitters of recognition across his skin. From the rapid-fire instructions, he knew even before he approached the trauma bay that the patient had just arrived. Even more surprising was that right in the center of the chaos, directing proceedings, was the brunette from the parking lot.

The attending physician.

He didn't know why the sight of her so competently handling the emergency threw him but it did—enough that he paused at the entrance, his gut clenching in a combination of dread and anticipation.

The kid, probably no more than six or seven, looked so tiny and fragile on the bed that he felt his heart squeeze before he had a chance to take an emotional step back. These were the cases that ripped at him. And he'd feel it all the more deeply if his team wasn't successful in reattaching the severed limb.

The sight of the blood-soaked compression dressing instantly sucked him back to West Africa where he'd spent the past two years replanting limbs torn off in explosions and artillery fire or lopped off by *panga*-wielding soldiers. The young victims had been the hardest to deal with because often there had been no limbs to reattach, or necrosis and infection had already set in by the time they got to him.

It meant a lifetime of unnecessary pain, suffering and disability—if they survived—and it made him wonder what the hell it was all for.

Lost in horrific memories, he scarcely heard the attending ask, "Who's the ortho on duty? Has someone called?"

It was only when he heard his name that he was jolted back to reality.

"Rona said Dr. St. James is on his way."

Momentarily rattled by the abrupt shift from memories that were still far too fresh and vivid in his mind to the bright lights of the trauma bay, Dylan watched her frown and pull the stethoscope from around her neck.

"Isn't that the new guy everyone's swooning over?" she asked absently, fitting the scope in her ears and sliding the metal disc over the boy's chest. Without waiting for an answer, she addressed the second nurse. "Paula, we're going to need more blood before we can get him into surgery. Set up another bag and make sure we have enough on standby. Let's hope Hot New Guy's not just a pretty face. The last thing *this* little guy needs is to grow up without an arm."

Taking a deep breath, Dylan shoved the memories aside and stepped into the room as she turned to the monitor.

Removing the stethoscope, she impatiently slung it around her neck. "Dammit, where *is* he? Amy, call him again. We—"

"No need," he interrupted, his eyes already assessing the boy's condition as he reached out and pressed his fingers against the brachial artery above the boy's severed arm. It was slow and ragged, barely there.

Hyper-aware of her just two feet away, he knew the instant she recognized him by her audible inhalation. His peripheral vision caught the way her body stilled and he looked up into eyes wide with shocked recognition.

Holding her gaze, he kept his voice low and soothing. "What kind of injury do we have, Dr...? Uh... Stevens, is it?"

"I… I…" she stuttered.

Dylan didn't know whether to feel pleased or insulted that she appeared so rattled. The blond nurse must have also noticed her reaction because her gaze narrowed, bouncing between them as though she sensed the abrupt tension in the room.

"Dani?" the nurse said, not pausing in bagging the intubated child. "You okay?"

The words clearly jolted her and she abruptly blinked, going from in control to flustered in the blink of an eye. "He's…uh…he…um—" She frowned and firmed her soft mouth as she visibly pulled herself together. "He lost his arm an inch above the left epicondyle."

The nurses looked at her in surprise before sharing a significant look.

"I can see that," he said quietly, ignoring the silent exchange. "Did the EMTs say how it happened?"

A flush stained her cheeks and she grimaced before sucking in a steadying breath. In the blink of an eye she was once again the cool, collected physician. "Apparently a plate glass window fell on him," she reported briskly, with only the barest hint of a tremor.

"Is it a crush injury?"

"No," she clipped out. "Fairly clean. I…uh… I had to clamp the brachial artery to raise his pressure but I'm not sure how much longer he can wait for surgery."

She'd made the right call. He nodded to the cooler on a nearby trolley. "What's the condition of the arm?"

"I haven't had a chance to look but the EMT said it's intact."

He lifted the blood-soaked compression bandage and noticed that a clamp had been applied to the end of the artery. After a quick assessment of the splintered edges of the bone, he gave a short nod as he turned to head for the door.

"Take X-rays of both sections and bring him up as soon as he's ready. We'll be waiting."

On his way up to surgery, he punched in a number on his phone.

"Kate," he said, when the doctor answered on the third ring. "It's Dylan—how soon can you get to OR?"

"About twenty minutes to a half-hour, why?"

"I need your needlepoint skills for a replantation."

The older doctor gave a low laugh. "I'm not on call, Dylan."

"I know," he admitted. "But when a kid loses his arm you're my go-to vascular. I need you on my team."

He heard her suck in a sharp breath. "A kid? Please don't tell me it's a crush injury."

He pressed the button to call for the elevator. "It's not a crush injury. A sheet of plate glass lopped off his arm an inch above the elbow. There's some damage, obviously but it should be straightforward."

He heard her sigh. "All right—start without me. I'm on my way."

While he waited for the elevator, he paged the on-call vascular surgeon, as well as a plastic surgeon. Once the elevator arrived he stepped inside, his mind already on the procedure ahead rather than the woman he'd left in the ER.

There would be time enough later to think about his reaction to seeing her again—that one-two punch he'd taken to the chest when those startled gray eyes had locked with his. She'd looked stunned and flustered, as though she hadn't expected to see him again. And a bit dismayed—which she hadn't been quick enough to conceal.

He'd felt kind of stunned himself and it wasn't because one glance into those smoky eyes had dropped the bottom out of his gut. *What the hell had that been about?*

No, he assured himself, he'd just been surprised. Surprised at finding her directing proceedings without any trace of the charming clumsiness she'd displayed at their first meeting. Yep—just surprise at finding her without even trying, he told himself.

It couldn't possibly be that when he'd seen her something deep inside him had stilled and said, *There you are.*

Because that would be crazy when there wasn't a hint of insanity in his family tree.

When the elevator doors opened, Dani and the RN pushed the gurney out and rushed it down the hallway to Surgery. She'd left Amy behind in the ER, taking care of their little patient's distraught mother, who'd arrived just as they were getting into the elevator.

Seeing her baby lying almost lifeless on the large, adult-sized bed had been almost too much for pregnant Christine Nolan. Dani had told Amy to give her something to calm her down before they had two patients on their hands.

The instant they pushed the gurney through the swing doors an OR nurse grabbed the cooler. "Room Four," she rapped out briskly. "They're waiting."

They quickly maneuvered down the passage to where a scrub nurse was holding the doors open, and even as she released the gurney Dani found her gaze drawn, despite herself, to the team gathered around the wall screen, studying the X-rays she'd taken ten minutes earlier.

Or rather her gaze was drawn inexorably toward one team member in particular.

As though sensing her presence, he turned, his gaze locking unerringly on to her. She ignored the way her pulse leapt at the sight of him, standing head and shoulders above everyone else in the room. Already dressed in his surgical scrubs, gowned and bandanna-ed, Dr. Hot-and-Hunky looked as if he owned his universe.

And was ready to rock hers.

Her face burned with mortification at the memory of their last two encounters and she hoped she could keep from humiliating herself a third time. What must he be thinking? she wondered. First, that she was clumsy and blurted out whatever came into her head; and second that she'd heard that deep bedroom voice of his and everything in her had come to a screeching halt.

She'd looked up into moss-green eyes surrounded by long, dark lashes and her mind had gone blank as a slate. And then he'd asked her about the wound and she'd replied with something so inane even a second-year med student would have blinked.

She just hoped no one had noticed and cringed because she knew everyone *had*. Especially him. *Oh God*, she thought as a fresh wave of embarrassment crawled up the back of her neck. She'd stood there frozen as if she was a teenager again and had found herself face to face with the hottest bad boy in school.

Realizing she was *still* standing there, Dani spun away to make a quick escape. She was almost through the doors when his voice—deep and dark and sinful—reached her.

"Dr. Stevens?"

Tempted to ignore him, she shoved aside the primitive urge to run and turned slowly, giving herself time to school her expression. She was a thirty-year-old professional, she reminded herself. She sucked in a steadying breath, hoping he couldn't see her inner chaos and terrified because she'd never been any good at hiding her emotions.

She just hoped she could keep her mouth from blurting out embarrassing inanities. "Yes?"

His gaze swept over her face to linger on her mouth and for one horrifying instant she thought he would mention their first meeting or...or even worse...ask about her unprofessional behavior in the ER.

Actually, no. Worse would be that he somehow *knew* that her first impulse had been to check her hair and straighten her posture. Fortunately she'd done neither. *Unfortunately* she'd embarrassed herself and surprised her colleagues by staring at him as though he'd popped through a tear in the space time continuum dressed like a Roman centurion.

Heck, even *that* wouldn't have shocked her as much.

He lifted a hand and, startled, she jerked back a couple of steps until her back hit the wall, her eyes wide. Embarrassment crawled up the back of her neck when she realized he was just scratching his jaw.

Way to totally overreact there, Dani.

She hastily glanced around to see if anyone had seen that clumsy panicked retreat and nearly sagged with relief when she saw that no one was paying them any attention.

Get a damn grip, Dani.

Concern darkened his gaze. "You okay?"

"Of course," she managed coolly. "Just in a hurry to…uh…" She gestured behind her. "Get back to the ER."

After a short pause he nodded, his eyes dropping briefly to the pulse tapping out frantic Morse code in her throat. She had to battle an overwhelming urge to cover that revealing little sign of agitation.

"Anything I should know about the boy?"

His deep voice, pouring over her like a benediction, should have relaxed her but instead it ratcheted her tension up a hundred notches.

"Allergies, medical conditions, any medication that he's on?"

"Uh…no," she said, clearing her throat. "His name is Timothy Nolan and he's seven years old. His mother says he's a normal, active little boy who loves ice hockey and dinosaurs. He's a Canucks supporter."

A smile lit his ruggedly handsome features, stealing her breath and sending her pulse lurching around like a drunken sailor on shore leave. When her knees gave an alarming wobble, she snapped her spine straight.

Stop looking at his smile, she snarled silently. *Handsome guys who flash million-dollar smiles can't be trusted. So walk away, nice and calm.*

"Well, we'll have to see that he gets to play hockey someday."

Relief that he wasn't going to mention her recent lapses almost had her knees buckling again.

That's good, Dani. Focus on your patient and not on your queasy stomach and wobbly knees.

"You can replant?" It could simply be the adrenaline let-down that was making her shaky and hyper-aware.

"The X-rays look good," he said and though she understood what he wasn't saying, she pressed on, "So Timmy will be normal again?"

He sent her a pained look and sighed. "I'll give it my best shot but I'm not a miracle-worker."

"That's not what I hear," she clipped out, almost rudely and flushed when one eyebrow rose up his forehead at her snippy tone.

But she wasn't about to be intimidated—not like that day almost sixteen years ago when another bad boy had caught her fascinated stare and with a slow smile had propped his shoulder against her locker. Leveling her with a sleepy, knowing look, he'd drawled, "Think you can handle what I've got, little girl?" and roared with laughter when she'd turned tail and bolted.

She felt exactly like that now but managed to lock her knees before they ignored the imperative from her brain to stand firm. She held his gaze a little defiantly.

His brow wrinkled, as though her behavior surprised him.

No more than it was surprising the hell out of her too.

After a short pause he repeated, "We'll do our best."

She gave a curt nod and had turned to go again when his voice called her softly.

"Dr. Stevens?" He waited until her gaze met his. "Don't believe everything you hear."

Dani got the feeling he was talking about more than just the hospital gossip that had him sleeping with more women than there were days in the month. And *that* was only since his return. Not only was she sure the rumors were grossly exaggerated but she hadn't received any creepy vibes from him.

Maybe not but you didn't get any creepy vibes from Richard either, a little voice of reason reminded her. *At least, not before the wedding. And look how that turned out.*

When she didn't respond, Dr. St. James sighed and looked as if he wanted to say something more. She braced herself, ignoring the way her pulse increased.

But then the anesthetist called his name and all he said was, "I have to go."

And look at that. She could feel the rush of disappointment that he hadn't...*what*? Pushed her up against the wall and put his hands and mouth all over her?

Sheesh, woman. Get a grip. This is a surgical suite. And maybe you could stop looking at his mouth and remember that you're on sabbatical from men. Remember why you've given them up.

She turned away abruptly, determined to leave with her dignity intact but yet again his voice—a rough slide of velvet against her skin—stopped her in her tracks.

"Oh, and Dr. Stevens…?"

Awareness skated across her and she wanted more than anything to escape.

He waited until she looked back before drawling softly, "I'm *not* just a pretty face."

She was embarrassed that he'd heard what she'd said in the ER but pride stiffened her spine and had her lying smoothly. "I wouldn't know."

She relaxed, inordinately pleased that she could be cool and professional—or at least pretend to be—beneath that intense green gaze. His hypnotic eyes held her hostage for a moment longer, then he nodded brusquely and turned away.

Before the door swung shut behind her she could hear the steady beeping of the monitors over her thundering pulse and she said a quick prayer for little Timmy—and one for the steady hands of those he'd been placed in.

Once in the elevator, away from prying eyes—especially intense green ones that seemed to see right through her—she sagged against the wall and locked her knees to keep from sliding to the floor. Pressing a shaky hand to her even shakier belly, she gave a ragged moan and banged her head against the side of the elevator a couple times, hoping to knock a little sense into her head.

Oh. My. God. She couldn't believe it. The guy she'd brushed off, then spent way too much time thinking about, was a surgeon...*at the very same hospital where she worked.* Not only *that*, he was the very same Dr. Hot Stuff all the female personnel—married *and* unmarried—were drooling over. And if *that* didn't have alarm bells shrieking away in the back of her mind, nothing would.

Not interested, she told herself firmly. She'd barely survived a relationship with one rich, handsome and hotly in demand man and she had no intention of melting for another.

Nope. No way. No how. Absolutely no melting.

But she'd *dreamed* about him, she was forced to admit. The type of dreams a girl never shared with *anyone*—not even her best friend. The types of dreams that made her blush just thinking about them, because she hadn't had a sexy dream since she was a shy, awkward teenager mooning over hot bad boys.

She would rather step in front of a bus than have him suspect that she was like every other woman, swooning when he turned his green eyes her way, ramping up her hormones while every nerve-ending, every strand of DNA, perked up and did a Mexican wave.

Look at me! her nipples had yelled.

The elevator doors opened and she was hugely relieved that the hallway was empty and she could enjoy her little freak-out in private. Instead of heading for the ER, she ducked into the bathroom and barely resisted the urge to shove her entire head under the cold water tap and drown herself.

She splashed her hot face instead and when she caught sight of her flushed cheeks and bright eyes, paused to give herself a stern lecture. *No brooding over hot, sexy surgeons with green eyes*, she told her reflection firmly. *At least until you can behave like a mature professional.*

On second thought, she should just stay away from the entire species altogether. Besides, he had even more women throwing themselves at him than Richard Ashford-Hall III. She wasn't *ever* going to be one of a crowd again. She would never put herself in a position where she had to fight for any man's attention. It was too humiliating to discover that no matter what you did you'd just never measure up.

Besides, she was damaged goods, wasn't she? And no man, Richard had told her cruelly, wanted damaged goods. If she couldn't do what she'd been put on the earth for—provide him with an heir—she was no good to anyone.

CHAPTER THREE

DESPITE THE FREQUENTLY frustrating cases and long, exhausting hours, Dani loved the ER. She loved the adrenaline and the challenge of emergency medicine; of saving lives and solving puzzling symptoms before her patients were transferred to the right specialist.

She dealt with new cases, new patients, all the time, and though it made for an exciting profession, she sometimes missed knowing what had happened to the critical patients she'd treated— missed the relationship that developed between patient and healthcare professional.

Sometimes the people they revived in the ER didn't make it, and sometimes they went on to live long, happy lives—she liked to think because her knowledge, skill and training had made it possible. But it was cases like little Timothy Nolan that grabbed her and didn't let go. It became a necessity, driven by some deep inner need, for her to follow up.

So when she heard that he was finally out of surgery Dani took advantage of the usual Thursday night lull and headed for the elevators, pressing the button for the tenth floor when the doors swished open.

She wanted to see for herself that he was okay, that everything she'd done for him had been enough to save his arm. *That*, she admitted to herself, was always a worry. That she'd done enough, done her best…when sometimes her best wasn't always enough.

But at least Timmy was healthy, and the hands he'd been passed on to skilled. The best, according to the grapevine in Vancouver. She didn't know if that was fact, or just the opinion of too many starry-eyed women.

It was after two-thirty a.m. when she headed down the passage toward Pediatric ICU, hearing the thin wail of a terrified child punching through the stillness. She spared a moment to think about the parents of that sick child and what they must be going through. And if she grieved the fact that she would never experience those highs and lows of parenthood for herself, she shoved it deep where it couldn't hurt.

It couldn't hurt as long as she didn't think

about it. And she'd certainly become adept at ignoring things she couldn't change.

Something else she'd ignored was thinking about...*him*. Then she walked past the nurses' station and saw him, standing at the window of a small private room in the ICU. With his feet spread wide, one arm folded across his wide chest and the opposite elbow resting on his wrist, while long tanned fingers scratched his jaw, he looked big and tough and just a little bit dangerous.

Still dressed in black scrubs, the soft material stretched across the width of his shoulders, he might have been an intimidating figure if not for the dark strands of hair sticking up in places, as though he'd spent the night shoving his fingers through it.

The rasp of his fingers against the eight-hours-past-five-o'clock shadow had her steps faltering along with her pulse. Her breath caught and for one panicked moment she wanted to turn and bolt before he saw her. But then common sense reasserted itself. She was entitled to check on a patient who had gone through her trauma bay. Besides, now that she'd seen him she was prepared. She was fine. She was—

His head turned abruptly and she felt pinned to the spot by the force of that laser-sharp gaze. She froze, and for just a split second his expression remained closed, intense and just a little bit somber. Her pulse lurched for another reason altogether and she felt her gut clench.

Oh God, something had gone wrong.

Then he blinked and the intensity cleared. A gleam of…well, something she wasn't ready to identify, lightened his gaze.

Rubbing her chilled arms, she took those last dozen steps toward him. "You look tired," she said quietly, a little jitter sneaking through her when one dark brow arched.

"I do?"

"Tired…" She forced her gaze to search his. "But satisfied."

Feeling inordinately proud that she'd managed a coolly professional observation when she was feeling so self-conscious, she turned to look through the window to where a young couple stood huddled by the bed, their expressions filled with a desperate kind of love. Her gaze went unerringly to the boy's left arm, swathed from shoulder to wrist in bandages. The small fingers

looked swollen but the color was pink enough
for relief to relax her shoulders.

"It went well?"

He shoved his hands into the pockets of his
scrubs pants and rocked back on his heels.
"Yeah…" he murmured.

Out of the corner of her eye she saw him turn
to look at her, and steeled herself against that
perceptive probe that seemed to see everything
she wanted to hide.

Keeping her attention locked on the little family of three and her expression bland, she challenged softly, "So…he'll be able to play for the
Canucks one day?"

His laugh was a rough slide of velvet against
nerve-endings scraped raw by the past, the late
hour and the reluctant knowledge that she was attracted—completely against her will—to a man
who made her ex seem like an unpopular loner.

The self-deprecating amusement in its deep
sound had Dani's gaze jumping to his. He looked
mildly disconcerted, as though she'd surprised
him but that was probably just a trick of the light.
Surgeons—especially the hot, hunky ones—
tended to think they had a private line to God.

"You don't ask for much, do you?"

"Are you telling me the rumors are wrong and you *are* just a pretty face?"

The look he sent her was filled with an irritated kind of exasperation. "What did I tell you about listening to gossip, Dr. Stevens?" he demanded, taking her arm and steering her to the door. "And, for your information, men aren't... *pretty.*"

No, she thought, that square jaw, the bold slash of his cheekbones and the high, broad forehead could hardly be called anything as frivolous as "pretty." He was too strong for that, too virile. But there was no doubt he was a ruggedly handsome man—a man with the kind of masculine sexuality that made women weak at the knees.

And in the head, she reminded herself.

He looked so pained that Dani would have grinned if she hadn't been blinking in surprise at finding herself expertly maneuvered out of Pediatric ICU toward the bank of elevators.

She stopped abruptly, wondering how it had happened. "What are you doing?"

He paused to grin down at her and she had to steel herself against the impulse to return it. *Dammit*, she thought, *he's sneaky.*

"I'm going to buy you dinner."

Her eyes narrowed in suspicion. "Dinner?"

The door opened behind them and a couple of nurses emerged, their curious gazes taking in the long fingers wrapped around her upper arm and the almost intimate familiarity of their bodies.

Fighting embarrassment, Dani edged away. The last thing she needed was to be linked even casually to Dr. Hot-and-Hunky.

He muttered a curse and dropped his hand as well as his voice, turning away even as he nodded at the women. "Yeah, you know... That meal you eat at the end of the day."

"It's three a.m.," she felt compelled to point out, ignoring the jitter in her belly.

His grin was lightning-fast. "Yeah, and I'm starving. So how about it? I know this great place in the West Wing that serves turkey sandwiches and hot coffee any time of the day or night. The atmosphere isn't the best but at least it'll be quiet this time of night."

And that was kind of the problem, she decided. The quiet intimacy of the twenty-four-hour bistro on the ground floor was a far cry from the bright cafeteria in the East Wing. Then there was being alone with him in a dim booth... Something that smacked of a date—something she'd avoided since her divorce.

"I'm on shift," she hedged, determined not to spend any more time in his company than was professionally necessary. "I just came up to see how Timmy was doing before heading back."

He punched the call button. "He's doing better than expected but only time will tell." He leaned against the wall and studied her with an unreadable gaze. "But then, you already know that."

She inclined her head in agreement, pretending he wasn't making her nervous. "So, how is the ER?" he asked, his eyes taking on a glint of amusement. As though he knew exactly what he was doing to her.

"Hopping," she replied, feeling her eyelashes flutter and cursing the faint heat climbing up her neck into her face. "Which is why I should hurry back."

His lips twitched and amusement gleamed in the gaze holding hers. "It's like a morgue down there, isn't it?"

Caught out in her lie, Dani rubbed her nose and contemplated lying again. The elevator arrived and she stepped inside. He followed, punching the ground-floor button before leaning back against the wall. When she avoided looking at him he chuckled, the sound low and deep in the confined space. Finally, she couldn't stand the suspense and sneaked a peek at him—which he caught. His brow arched, his eyes filling with amused knowledge of her prevarication.

She sighed. "How did you know?"

"I remember my ER rotation and…" He hitched a shoulder, the move straining the seams of his scrub top. "You're here. If it was hopping you would have waited until the end of your shift to check up on me. Make sure I know what I'm doing."

Unable to dispute his logic, Dani rolled her eyes and reminded him smartly, "I'm taking a break."

"From Y-chromosomes or from the ER?"

He gave a crooked smile that was entirely too casual and appealing for her peace of mind. It left her jittery because… Dammit, she didn't know the *because*. And that was what worried her.

"It's just coffee and turkey sandwiches with a colleague," he said, following her out of the elevator when the doors swished open on the ground floor. "Besides, I thought you'd want to know how the surgery went."

* * *

Danielle Stevens looked at him out of the corner of her suspicious eye. He could practically see the wheels grinding away in her head and he bit back a smile. If he'd wanted to delay her departure, he couldn't have picked a better way.

She frowned. "You want to discuss your patient with me?"

"Your patient too," he reminded her cheerfully, telling himself that she wasn't really his type and wondering why he was suddenly so sure that she was. She wasn't beautiful—at least not in a classic way—and she wasn't sophisticated. But there was just something so… *appealing* about her that his gaze kept being drawn back despite himself.

She'd shoved the jumbled mass of her dark curls into a messy topknot that left tendrils escaping every which way. Her nails were short and round and though she wore no rings, her hands were long and elegant, as though they were meant to wear beautiful things. She wore no make-up except a swipe of mascara on those long, lush lashes as a careless nod to feminine vanity.

He dropped his eyes to her wide, unpainted mouth, with its full bottom lip and slightly longer upper lip, and wondered if it was as soft as it looked…if it tasted as sweet as he'd dreamed.

She shook her head. "Not anymore." A long curl swung against her cheek and she brushed it aside with unconscious impatience. "Not once I sign off."

And then there was all that wary mistrust in her heavily fringed gray eyes when she looked at him, as though she expected him to turn into a raging jerk. The women he dated—his usual type, he admitted wryly—were confident, sophisticated women who knew the score. Women who looked at him as if he was the next best thing to a Tiffany bracelet, not as if she expected him to grow fangs and snarl.

From the looks of Dr. Danielle Stevens, she didn't know there *was* a score and would probably back away from a sparkly bauble as though it might bite her…as though *he* might bite her.

He had to admit that he was tempted to sink his teeth into that wide, soft mouth. Just to taste, he assured himself, even though he knew he was lying.

He wanted more than a taste of Danielle Stevens.

She intrigued him, balancing a determined

efficiency with something soft and fragile. She was both tough and gentle, sweet and tart. And beneath the smell of disinfectant he detected the warm scent of woman with a trace of cool freshness. It reminded him of a forest on a hot day—cool, mysterious and more than a little intriguing. It made him want to bury his face in her neck and breathe it into his lungs, to see if she tasted as cool and fresh as she smelled.

Which startled him. Because he couldn't ever remember wanting to smell a woman's neck before. Or at least not with such...*need*. The thought surprised him, because it had been a long time since he'd needed anything. Especially a woman.

He paused and pushed open the door to the bistro just as her phone rang, and if he hadn't been studying her with such brooding intensity he might have missed the odd expression that flitted across her face as she checked the screen.

Dylan swallowed a chuckle because although she'd frowned down at the caller ID she hadn't been entirely successful in masking her relief.

It was the second time a phone call had interrupted his plans for the night, he admitted ruefully but although he'd been relieved by the first, he couldn't help feeling just a little frustrated now the shoe was on the other foot. And did she *have* to look so damn eager to escape?

"I have to go," she said, using almost the exact words he'd used to his mother.

And without waiting for a response from him she turned and hurried away. Leaving him for the second time in less than a week to watch her walk away.

Realizing that he was watching the way her hips swayed—the sweet curve of her bottom in the shapeless scrubs and the long, slender legs eating up the distance—Dylan pressed his thumb and forefinger against his tired eyes and dragged air into his lungs.

It appeared he'd just discovered a weakness for sweet, sassy brunettes with sad gray eyes and a penchant for clumsiness.

Oh, yeah, he thought with a chuckle. Dylan St. James was a goner.

Dani pushed open the employees' door to find the city bathed in bright early-morning light. It had been a crazier than normal Friday night.

Aside from the rogues' gallery—drunk idiots who had been left to sleep off their stupidity—her most challenging case had been a middle-aged high society woman with a bunch of puzzling symptoms. It had turned out she'd unwittingly taken a cannabis overdose from helping herself to her nephew's marijuana cookies. And, while it had taken most of the night, a whole bunch of tests and a lot of frustration, it had been satisfying to discover that her instincts about it not being a brain tumor or a heart problem had been spot-on.

Recalling what the shift supervisor had said about the full moon, Dani turned in a circle to study the sky. Either Rona had been mistaken or it had dipped behind the mountains.

"Whatcha looking at?" ER resident Theo Anderson demanded as he and Amy descended the stairs. He looked up to scan the clear sky. "A bird? A plane? Or maybe a flying squirrel?"

"Isn't that supposed to be Superman?" she murmured, reaching up to pull the band from her hair and shake out the heavy, messy mass.

"Not in Vancouver," Theo said with a headshake, slinging an arm around her shoulders. "But I can be your hero, if you like."

Laughing, Dani shoved him away. "I'm good."

She gave in to a huge yawn, dreaming about hot food, hot coffee, a hot shower and her bed.

She wasn't dreaming about a hot man. *Nuh-uh. Nope.* Because they were the worst kind of trouble.

"No heroes required," she said, because she didn't need rescuing.

Okay, she *mostly* didn't need rescuing, she amended silently. Especially by someone who reminded her that she was a red-blooded woman.

Out of the corner of her eye she caught Amy studying her with a concerned frown. "You *do* know that not all guys are like your ex, don't you?"

Hiding a grimace, because the last thing she wanted was to discuss her past on such a beautiful day, Dani watched Theo perform a magic trick for Wendy, a pediatric night nurse, and murmured, "I know that. Some of them are like Theo."

Amy snorted and pulled her sunglasses from her bag. "Okay, so I can totally see why you're off guys." Her smile faded. "But you can't hide forever, Dani. It's not healthy."

"I'm not hiding," Dani argued. "I just haven't met anyone who's tempted me, that's all."

Instantly an image of a tall surgeon with hot green eyes, a sexy mouth and big warm hands popped into her head, and suddenly she was experiencing the kind of shiver that made some women pull out their lip gloss and check their hair.

Fortunately she wasn't one of those women. Mentally crossing her fingers, because she wasn't *usually* one of those women, she said, "When the right guy comes along I'll go for it, I promise."

Yeah, like you did last week...and the other night?

Shut up, she told the voice, pushing out her bottom lip to blow an impatient breath.

"You thought Richard was Mr. Right," Amy pointed out with a logic that Dani would have liked to dispute but couldn't.

Okay, maybe she hadn't thought he was the *right* guy but she'd been embarrassingly geeky and inexperienced. He'd been the first guy to pay her any real attention and she'd been hugely flattered that someone as handsome and popular as Richard had been interested in *her.*

Probably the reason she'd fallen so fast and so hard.

"Maybe you should look for Mr. Wrong instead?" Amy suggested. "Get out of your head and have a little fun for a change."

Before she could respond, Theo called out, "We're heading for Harry's tonight. You two coming?"

Dani shook her head, glad of the opportunity to escape because once Amy got her teeth into something, she rarely let it go. "I've got a thing."

"A thing?" Amy demanded, her brow arched skeptically. "What thing?"

Yeah, Dani. What thing?

She shrugged helplessly, too tired to think up a legitimate excuse. "A *thing* thing."

Amy narrowed her eyes and pointed accusingly at Dani. "There—see. That's exactly what I'm talking about."

She blinked. "Huh?"

"You're allergic to fun."

Dani couldn't help feeling a little insulted as she stared at her friend. Was that how people saw her? "I'm fun," she argued. "I go out with you guys all the time—and wasn't it just last month that you had to stop me from dancing on the tables at The Gateway?"

"No, that was Wendy and Theo," Amy said dryly.

She grimaced. *Oh, right.*

"Dani," Amy said gently. "When was the last time you actually went on a *date* date? You know—with a guy you're attracted to?"

"I'm not ready to date."

Heck, she recalled with an inner wince, just the thought of having coffee and a sandwich with a colleague in a dim bistro had thrown her for a loop. She didn't want to know how she'd handle a *real* date.

Okay, so she *did* know. She'd panic and run— she winced again—like that geeky fourteen-year-old she'd once been. It was kind of embarrassing that she was still letting hot boys scare her.

Amy studied Dani with narrowed eyes. "Then maybe you can explain exactly what happened the other night with Dr. Hunky?"

Her belly clenched and then released but it was an effort to appear casual. "I don't know what you're talking about," Dani said absently, digging in her bag for her sunglasses. "I was expecting Steve Randall and I was...surprised. That's all."

Yeah, right. Shocked was a little closer to the truth.

"Hmm..." Amy said, with enough skepticism

to have Dani, who was now pretending to look for her car keys, look up with a frown.

"What's that supposed to mean?" she demanded.

For a couple of seconds Amy looked conflicted, before she sighed. "I wasn't going to say anything," she began reluctantly. "But I heard that you and Dr. Hot Stuff were seen outside PICU the other night, looking pretty cozy."

Dani felt her jaw drop. "Wha—?" she spluttered, feeling her face heat. "Th—that's ridiculous. We were discussing Timmy Nolan and..." She spluttered. "I don't even *know* him."

Amy's answer was to raise her eyebrows. "Then why are you blushing?"

"Blu—? Of course I'm not blushing!" she yelped, her blush deepening at the sight of Amy's arched brows. "I'm annoyed that people haven't got anything better to do than gossip."

Amy snorted. "Annoyed? That a hot, sexy guy had his hands on you and was looking at your mouth?" One eyebrow rose up her forehead. "Yeah, I can totally see how you'd be *annoyed*."

Dani's eyes widened and the base of her spine tingled. *He'd been looking at her mouth?*

At the expression on her face, Amy cracked

up. "You should see your face," she hooted, almost rubbing her hands together with glee. "You *so* have the hots for the big bad boy of Ortho."

With a dirty look, Dani pulled out her keys and stomped across the parking lot toward her car. She wasn't going to dignify that with an answer because there was no way she had the hots for anyone. Let alone the big bad— She stopped and snorted rudely.

Who the heck talked like that, anyway?

CHAPTER FOUR

DANI PARKED A couple of blocks from the marina so she could hit the supermarket. And, although she'd had every intention of walking right on by, before she knew it she was standing inside her favorite coffee shop, breathing in the heady scent of freshly brewed coffee and thinking she'd gone to heaven.

Owen Lawrence, the owner, looked up when Dani pressed her nose up against the display case and moaned. "Need a moment there, hon?"

Dragging her gaze away from the rows of freshly baked temptation, she laughed. "Hi, Owen. And, no—it's just been a *very* long night."

Jeez, had she just moaned?

Maybe Amy was right. Maybe she *did* need to get a life—especially since the closest thing she'd come to sex in years had been that full-body shiver she'd experienced when she'd walked into PICU the other night and seen a certain surgeon standing there, looking like the answer to some-one's hot dream.

Not hers, of course. But someone's…

"Crazy night?"

She smothered a yawn. "You wouldn't believe *half* the stuff we get in the ER on Friday nights."

Pretending she wasn't coveting the deca-dent pastries, Dani waited in line and casually glanced around at the patrons getting an early start to their weekend. An elderly couple sat nearby, holding hands and smiling, content to be in each other's company.

Before she could stop it, her mouth curved in an answering smile and if she felt a little pang, a little pinch right beside her heart. It wasn't that she was jealous. She was just… *Dammit*, she wanted that when she was their age too.

Heck, she wouldn't mind something like that at *her* age but she'd tried and it hadn't worked out. In fact it had left her with far more than a few emotional scars. Scars that ached now, at the sight of a young couple at the next table, laugh-ing and fussing over a cooing baby in a stroller. Hidden physical scars that made having a per-fect little family of her own just a pipe dream.

But that was okay, she told herself, ignoring

the impulse to rub the ache where a child of her own would never grow. There were worse things than being unable to conceive. For one: being married to a man who believed he was entitled to jet-set off to exotic locations with models, actresses, friends... In fact any woman—single or married—who wasn't his wife.

Richard had been movie-star-handsome, romantic and attentive—right up until they'd married. Almost immediately he'd become demanding and critical of everything she said, the way she behaved and what she wore. Then had come the subtly cruel remarks and finally, after a year, the emotional abuse had turned into towering rages that often erupted into bouts of violence. She'd lived in a constant state of tension and hated to think how easily she'd been cowed.

Although he'd never actually hit her until that last so-called "business" weekend—the one that had ended not only her nightmare of a marriage but had caused her accident—he'd used his much larger size to intimidate. To literally push her around, grab her with hard, biting hands and knock her into things because he'd said he needed to knock sense into her.

She shuddered. She wouldn't *ever* live like that

again. Maybe she was still a work in progress but she was never going to let a man crush her spirit along with her shaky confidence in herself as a woman.

She was older and wiser now, and she knew better than to be swayed by a pretty face and an expensive smile. Knew better than to think she was equipped to handle Prince Not-So-Charming.

Or sexy bad boys with hot green eyes that saw way too much.

Suppressing a shiver, Dani paid for her coffee and splurged on the biggest chocolate cream donut covered with chocolate ganache. Heading for the door, she took a huge bite of the sinful delight even before her foot hit the sidewalk.

She was so focused on stuffing her face with the melt-in-the-mouth donut and double-shot latte that she wasn't paying much attention to her surroundings—until two pre-teens on skateboards nearly knocked her off her feet.

"Watch it, lady!" they warned cheerfully, performing a perfect whatever before zipping off.

"*You* watch it," she yelled to their departing backs, before looking at where her half-eaten breakfast lay partly on the sidewalk and partly down the front of her scrubs. She was now wearing her coffee and a blob of chocolate cream.

"*Dammit.* I needed that."

With a sigh, she scrubbed at the stain with the paper napkin, mourning the loss of her coffee. Picking up the empty to-go cup and the rest of the donut, she tossed everything in the nearest trash bin and told herself it was just as well because she really *didn't* need the extra bazillion calories.

Muttering to herself, Dani turned to head for the supermarket—and walked into a wall of muscle and bone. The abrupt interruption of her forward momentum drew a startled squeak from her parted lips and she lurched backward, just as large hands closed over her upper arms to keep her from the same fate as her breakfast.

"Careful," a deep voice cautioned.

And when that smooth yet velvet-rough voice—that *familiar* velvet-rough voice—rumbled near her ear her head came up, the automatic apology dying in her throat. "Dr. St. J-James, what—what are you doing here?"

His eyes took a leisurely journey over her face, lingering on her mouth for a long moment before dropping to the coffee and chocolate stain on the front of her scrubs top.

"Since we keep meeting like this you should probably call me Dylan," he said, and chuckled, brushing one hand down her arm as he looked past her shoulder to the coffee shop behind her. "Apparently I'm doing the same as you." He tugged gently at the damp fabric. "Although wearing my coffee wasn't quite what I had in mind."

"I wasn't looking where I was going and some kids—" She saw amusement crinkle the corners of his eyes and abruptly pressed her lips together to stop herself from babbling.

"Yeah, I saw," he murmured.

The brush of his fingers, the closeness of his big hard body, had the breath backing up in her throat. It was a couple of seconds before she realized that her nipples had drawn into tight little buds of enthusiastic greeting.

His gaze slowly rose up her chest, paused at the frantic pulse hammering against the delicate skin of her throat and then lifted to lock on to her eyes. The amusement had been replaced by a sizzling masculine heat that sent both panic and anticipation rolling across her skin.

Oh God. Oh God. Oh—

Realizing she was standing there, gaping at him, she said, "Um…" very intelligently, and then sucked in a steadying breath as she mentally scrambled to rein in her scattered wits. *Darn it*, what the heck *was* it about the guy that always caught her on the back foot, banished her IQ and reduced her to a stammering fourteen-year-old?

Whatever it was, she fumed, it was going to stop. *Right now.* All she had to do was remind him that she was still on the man wagon and—

"…breakfast?"

Dani blinked when she realized that he was talking and she'd totally missed it because she'd been gazing at his strong, tanned throat and wondering what it would feel like to press her lips there.

"Uh…excuse me?"

Amusement tugged at his mouth. One minute she was staring into smiling green eyes and the next, she felt her head go light, her knees buckle, just like all those swooning women who—

And then she was being thrust into a chair and her head shoved between her legs. The spots dancing in front of her eyes gradually faded and she became aware of his large, comforting presence beside her. The warm fingers on the back of her neck that kept her from sliding to the floor.

"I've never actually had someone fall at my feet before," he said chuckling, sounding just a little bit disgruntled.

She cracked open an eye to see him crouched beside her.

He dipped his head to catch her look. "I'm not so sure if it's a compliment."

All she could manage was a strangled laugh as heat and a mouth-watering masculine scent surrounded her, invading her lungs. He was close. *Too* darn close.

Her pulse gave an alarmed little blip and she jerked upright—or tried to—but his grip tightened.

"Take it easy," he murmured, his long fingers gentling to soothe the back of her head, to massage her neck and the tense spot between her shoulder blades.

Oh, that felt good.

"You fainted."

Fainted?

She shook her head in denial and opened her mouth to tell him she hadn't but a delicious heat had begun to invade her limbs, threatening to melt her bones. It occurred to her that if she didn't move soon she'd slide right off the chair into a puddle of yearning between his large, scuffed boots.

Oh, boy. Way to go on not embarrassing yourself.

She squeezed her eyes closed to dispel the swirling heat taking up residence in her belly, then sucked in a steadying breath before sitting up, stilling when she discovered him less than an inch away.

He'd recently shaved and the smell of soap and some manly scent—shaving gel…aftershave?—teased her nostrils. The shape of his mouth drew her gaze and she had the wildly inappropriate impulse to lean forward and lick it. The little flutter in her belly had her struggling to pull air into lungs that refused to work—probably because she was inhaling a heady mix of testosterone and male pheromones.

Long, tanned fingers cupped her jaw, sending a jolt right through her. Her gaze jumped to his as he swept concerned eyes over her face.

"You have a little more color in your cheeks," he murmured, his thumb gently rubbing a line of heat across her cheekbone.

It sent a bunch of conflicting signals to the rest of her body: delicious tingles, nervous jitters and an insidious softening in places that hadn't softened for a man in nearly three years.

And if *that* didn't freak her out, the way his eyes darkened had her swallowing a panicked gasp and hastily retreating. She started to pull away.

"Don't tense up," he instructed.

He spoke in a deep, exasperated voice that had Dani opening her mouth to croak, "I'm f-fine," before wrapping her fingers around his wrist to push him away.

She couldn't think when he was touching her.

He resisted a moment before dropping his hand. He didn't, however, move back, and her belly gave a decidedly nervous little feminine quiver.

Oh, boy. Bad time to rediscover her hormones.

"When last did you eat?"

She blinked. "What?" *She* was thinking about sex and *he* was thinking about…food?

A bubble of hysterical laugher rose up her throat. It figured, she thought with a snort. Just figured that her body would come out of the deep freeze at the exact moment the man in front of her was focused on food.

"When last did you eat?"

She looked down at the coffee stain on the front of her scrubs and tried to think. "I…uh…" *Damn*, she thought, shoving her hair out of her eyes with shaking fingers. She couldn't concentrate with him so close. "Last night…yesterday…"

She shook her head impatiently and tried to stand but he casually shoved her back.

"I can't remember exactly. The ER was busy. *Dammit*—will you *move*?" she growled, embarrassed by the curious glances they were receiving. "I can't b-breathe with you so close and…" She lowered her voice. "People are staring."

"Let them stare," he said impatiently, rising smoothly to his feet. "Stay there while I get you something."

She made a sound deep in her throat—kind of an annoyed growl and distressed squeak—and tried to stand again but his hand dropped to her shoulder to keep her seated. She jerked her head up and opened her mouth to snap at him but he swiped a casual thumb across her bottom lip. The move surprised her—okay, shocked the hell out of her—rendering her mute as well as brainless.

"Stay there," he murmured. "Please."

It seemed she wasn't as immune as she'd thought—or wanted to be. Not if she was unable to ignore a man who looked at her with amused exasperation and banked heat. "Okay…"

His eyes took on a challenging gleam as he tugged gently on an errant curl that had escaped her topknot. When his fingers slid away they brushed her neck, sending a host of sensations scattering throughout her body. Her nerves jittered, causing something deep in her belly to pull taut. It was probably a good thing she was sitting down because her knees wobbled alarmingly.

She pressed a shaky hand to her hollow belly and groaned. Oh God, maybe she *was* hungry. Maybe she just needed food.

Yeah, you're hungry, all right, said the voice in her head, snickering rudely. *Hungry for sinful se—*

Nope, she was still quite comfortable on the wagon, thank you very much. She had no intention—none whatsoever, she assured herself—of falling off for anyone.

Especially not a guy who wore his general hotness like a familiar well-loved T-shirt—one that stretched across his big shoulders, pulled taut over a wide muscular chest and fell loose around his abs and narrow waist before being tucked into low-slung jeans that were faded in strategic places and cupped some pretty cuppable places.

Her breath hitched and an unfamiliar burn took up residence in a place that had been empty for far too long. She shifted restlessly, because it made her uncomfortable and twitchy. And since being twitchy always made her irritable she decided it was probably way past time to hit the road.

Before the wagon rumbled on down the street without her.

Muttering to herself about the dangers of getting sucked into an Alpha man's orbit, she shoved back her chair—because the last thing she needed was nuclear blasts of testosterone and pheromones clouding her judgment and adding to her problems.

But before she could stand she caught a whiff of the sticky sweet scent of fresh donuts along with the aroma of hot vanilla bean latte and nearly moaned.

"Going somewhere?"

Looking up as Dr. St. James—*Dylan*—slid into the opposite chair, Dani's stomach lurched and rumbled simultaneously. She wasn't entirely certain if it was the sight of all that yumminess or the smell of coffee and donuts that had her subsiding back into the chair.

An eyebrow rose up his forehead as he slid a large to-go mug across the table. "Drink," he ordered. "And tell me why you were getting ready to ditch me again. You're starting to give me a complex."

Dani cursed her fair complexion that had heated guiltily at the mild censure in his voice. He sounded as though her reluctance had baffled or maybe hurt him. But, considering that he had dozens of women vying for his attention, the idea that she could hurt his feelings was laughable.

"No, I wasn't," she lied. "I was… I was about to come and help you," she finished lamely. "And the only 'complex' thing about a man is his DNA. And even *that's* been decoded."

He laughed. "Uh-huh?"

Rolling her eyes, she spied the box he'd opened and was nudging across the table as though it contained a bomb.

A box of donuts? Jeez. That was about a gazillion calories right there.

Her eyes narrowed accusingly because of course *he* didn't need to worry about whether his butt looked good in jeans. But, then again, he was the kind of man who'd look good in anything…and in nothing at all.

A shiver skated across her skin at the thought and she quickly looked away before he realized she'd just pictured him naked. He made a low, rough sound in the back of his throat and when she gave in to the need to look she saw he was studying her with that deeply intense gaze that seemed to see everything.

He inclined his head at the box, his eyes and his wicked grin daring her to give in to temptation.

She'd never been able to resist a challenge and, staring into his moss-green eyes, Dani felt tempted. *Really* tempted. For about a nanosecond. Because she had a feeling this sexy dare went beyond donuts and into the realms of her man embargo. No matter what she'd told Amy, she wasn't *nearly* ready to date and had a sneaky feeling she wouldn't *ever* be ready for a man like him.

He was too masculine, too sexy, too Alpha… Well, frankly he was too *everything*. All the things that hit her every button…including her inner alarm.

Dragging her eyes away from the open box, she scowled. "I'm abstaining, remember?"

Hitching one shoulder, as though her resistance didn't bother him, he leaned forward and selected a chocolate cream ganache-glazed donut. And then, with his gaze on hers, he said casually, "I thought that was just from anything with a Y-chromosome," before sinking strong white teeth into the fried dough.

Her belly quivered and her tongue emerged to swipe across her bottom lip as she imagined licking glaze—*Oh God*—and chocolate cream off his lips.

She must have made a sound, because his eyes darkened and dropped to her mouth.

"No," she said a little primly, even as she squirmed on the seat, feeling turned on and jealous of a greasy pillow of fried dough. *Sheesh.* She clearly needed to date more if the sight of a guy enjoying a donut was making her both resentful of the attention he was giving it as well as aroused. "From *everything* that's bad for me."

He chuckled and nudged the box closer. "C'mon, live a little. You need to stabilize your blood sugar and…" He paused, looking far too innocent. "Isn't it your duty as a healthcare professional to think about my arteries by taking one or two off my hands?"

No looking at his hands, Dani ordered herself, and then promptly did…and shivered as she recalled how those broad-palmed, long-fingered hands had felt rubbing away her tension.

"Why?" she demanded skeptically. "Afraid they'll go straight to your butt and you'll have to buy new jeans?"

His gaze dropped to her front, as though he could see through the table and she barely restrained herself from squirming. His amused snort said he thought she was joking when she'd been serious as a heart attack.

"No," he drawled softly, his mouth curving wickedly as though he'd been thinking of *her* bottom. "And neither should you."

His eyes dared her, and one arched brow accused her of being a wimp. She returned it with a glare, secretly pleased that he thought she didn't need to worry about getting a big butt.

"So," she said, lifting her cup to blow on the

hot liquid. "You want me to what…? Stay and help you empty the box?"

A self-deprecating smile tugged at his mouth. "I'll settle for feeding you before you pass out on me again. Not," he said, with a chuckle at her quick scowl, "that I object to getting my hands on you again but let's just say I find myself wanting to change your mind."

Ignoring the first part of his statement, she took a sip of latte to give herself a moment. "About…?"

His smirk grew. "You know what."

Dani's face bloomed with color as his meaning sank in. "I…um… I'm pretty sure that's not going to happen," she announced, rolling her eyes when he snorted.

Sheesh. Time to move the conversation into non-embarrassing territory.

"So…um…how's Timothy doing?"

He leaned back in the chair, looking relaxed and far too attractive so early in the morning—especially with her looking like week-old road-kill. His expression turned chiding and he looked just a little amused at her avoidance of a little harmless flirting.

"Remarkably well," he drawled. "Which you

know since you visited him last night and then again this morning."

She frowned at this news that he was keeping tabs on her but decided not to think about what it might mean. A smile bloomed at the memory of the little boy, almost bouncing off the walls with impatience. It was hard to believe he'd been at death's door just a couple days before.

"I did." She chuckled. "He wanted to know when Dr. Dylan was visiting, because apparently you'd promised to play catch with him."

"He's a cute kid," he said, his eyes taking on a little gleam she wanted to ignore. "And you're dodging the issue."

"What issue?" she asked politely, pretending to be clueless.

With a low laugh he shook his head at her and pushed the box closer. He took another bite of the donut he was still holding. "Go on," he urged, in a voice that was deep and sinful enough to tempt a nun to the dark side. "You know you want to."

And when she made a little distressed sound in the back of her throat because she was tempted— way too much and not just by the allure of fried dough—he snickered. *The jerk.*

"A little trans fat and a few empty calories once in a while won't hurt."

"Maybe not," she agreed. "But one always leads to two, and before you know it you've eaten the entire box and have to take up jogging to minimize the damage to your arteries...among other things."

"Are we talking about donuts or...?"

Her belly quivered at his implication but she ruthlessly squelched it. There would be no quivering. Not for him or anyone else. At least not until she had her life firmly in order.

"Yep," she said, making the *p* pop audibly. "Definitely donuts."

He chuckled, and with his eyes on hers stretched out his arm to hold the chocolate cream donut he'd just taken a bite of to her lips. "Why don't we share? That way you won't have to feel guilty."

And suddenly Dani wanted to step outside her safe, peaceful world. *Just once*, she told the voice in her head. Just once and then she'd go back to ignoring the way he made all the lonely little places inside her shiver with excitement.

Unable to look away, she leaned forward to sink her teeth into the sugary treat, very carefully avoiding taking a bite out of his finger too—which she was totally tempted to do.

Her taste buds instantly exploded and a vicious little tug deep in her belly drew her breasts tight, as though they were connected by some invisible thread. She must have made a sound, because his gaze rose slowly to hers, leaving a trail of fire streaking across her skin. The heat burning in the green depths had the breath backing up in her lungs.

She froze, her eyes widening. *Holy cow.* Whoever had said green eyes were hard and cold had never seen them catch fire. Her heart stuttered to a stop, because although she might not have seen it in a while there was no mistaking *that* look. The fact that it was focused on *her* had wild heat storming into her face.

Oh, no. No, no, *no*, she ordered herself frantically. No belly-clenching, knee-wobbling or heart-stuttering allowed. And if the alarming symptoms continued she'd head right back to the ER to order a full blood work-up…or maybe a neurological one.

She was far too smart to develop a…a *thing*— she wasn't going to call it an attraction—for Dylan St. James.

Wasn't she?

* * *

Without realizing he needed to, Dylan reached for her hand—and knew instantly that he'd made a tactical error when a jolt shot up his arm with a nasty little buzz. She must have felt it too, because her eyes widened and she gave a gasp of surprise.

Very interesting, he thought, narrowing his gaze on her startled expression. He'd heard about it, of course, but he'd never actually believed it existed. Nor had he ever experienced that sharp little zap of sexual heat.

Given the little bobble of shock that had nearly splashed hot liquid over the rim of her disposable cup, it appeared that neither had Danielle Stevens.

Eyes wide, wild color rushing beneath that soft skin, she jerked her hand free and quickly shoved it beneath the table to rub it against her thigh. Enjoying the sensations that little jolt had sent shooting up his arm, Dylan watched her struggle for composure, watched those wild fluctuations of color beneath her creamy skin.

Needing to put her at ease, he drew in a deep breath. "Danielle..." he began, pausing when she abruptly slapped her coffee cup onto the table and shoved back her chair.

"I…uh…oh, gosh, look at the time," she babbled, grabbing her shoulder bag as she lurched to her feet, almost toppling the chair in her haste.

He reached out to grab it before it crashed onto the floor and rose to his feet. She took a hasty step backwards, babbling out a garbled apology when she bumped into the table behind her.

"Look, don't g-get up," she stammered breathlessly as she edged away. "Enjoy your coffee and…and, thanks."

He started to follow her but she gave a little squeak of distress then turned and fled, leaving Dylan to watch in stunned surprise as she lurched her way between the tables to the door.

With a muttered and completely baffled curse, he followed. What the heck had he done to upset her? And she clearly *was* upset, because a woman didn't practically fall over herself trying to get away from a man for no reason.

He caught up with her a half-block from the coffee shop and grabbed her arm. "Dr. Stevens, wait—"

Wide-eyed, she spun around, wrapping her arms around her chest and curling her hands over her opposite elbows as though to protect herself from him. She was practically vibrating with tension.

Easily reading the wariness in her huge gray eyes, he slowly released her to shove his hands into his pockets. The last thing he wanted was to upset her—especially when his instincts were yelling at him to pull her close and not let go. He didn't think that would go down well.

"Hey...*hey*..." he crooned softly, cursing the caution in her storm-colored eyes and his own suddenly violent need. "It's okay." He gave her a crooked smile, hoping to draw one from her. "You can trust me. I'm a doctor."

The words had the desired effect, and with a muffled giggle she relaxed her shoulders. She drew in a deep breath and he watched her struggle to compose herself. He had to admire her grit, he told himself, because it was obvious that whatever—or *whoever*—had hurt her, they had done a really good job.

He hated thinking that some man had put his hands on her in anger but that was what all those little tells indicated. He'd grown up to respect women—his mother wouldn't have had it any other way—and to abhor bullies. A man who used physical violence on a woman or a child didn't deserve to be called a man.

"If that's the best you can do, Dr. St. James," she drawled, shoving her hair off her face with a hand that trembled, "I'm going to start questioning the rumors about your supposed reputation as a playboy."

"What have I told you about listening to gossip, Danielle?" he chided gently, relief settling around him like a sigh when she rolled her eyes. And when her mouth curved into a tiny smile, lighting those mysterious eyes, he felt as if he'd won a huge victory.

"Dani."

He blinked. "Huh?"

"It's Dani. With an i."

He took in the perfect oval of her face, the gray eyes, wide and heavily lashed beneath the elegant arch of her brows, the smooth curve of her cheek, the delicate nose and wide mobile mouth with its longer upper lip and pillow-soft bottom lip.

Dani sounded too masculine—too androgynous—he decided, for such a feminine face.

"Danielle suits you better," he announced, enjoying the way her creamy skin took on a rosy hue, as though she wasn't used to compliments.

"It does not," she countered, with a spluttered laugh. "Danielle evokes images of a tall, elegantly sophisticated French woman draped in silk and reeking of expensive perfume. *So* not me."

"Oh, I don't know…" he mused, casually nudging her behind a large pillar out of pedestrian traffic. "I kind of think it suits you."

He found himself needing to touch her but was hesitant about spooking her into bolting again. Testing the waters, he reached out to tug at an errant curl lying against her pale neck and was pleased to note that, other than a quick shiver, she didn't retreat.

"Yeah, right," she snorted, looking down at her attire. "Nothing says sophisticated elegance more eloquently than stained scrubs and battered running shoes." She lifted her head and arched her brow, still looking more like a Danielle than a Dani. "Be careful, Dr. St. James," she warned lightly. "Or people might think you've lost your touch."

Lost his mind, more likely, he thought with

an inner chuckle. Out loud, he said, "Spend the day with me."

"Yes... No... I... *What?*"

She gaped at him as though he'd suggested something indecent, when the truth was he wasn't ready to let her go. Wasn't ready for her to disappear on him again; leave him fighting that baffling desire to pull her close and kiss her senseless.

He moved a fraction closer and dropped his voice. "Spend the day with me, Dani with an i," he murmured. "I promise to feed you something that won't stain your scrubs or end up on your thighs."

She rolled her eyes. "Dr. St. James, I—"

Her eyes clouded and he watched her inner struggle.

Just when he thought she'd accept, she gave a quick head-shake and said regretfully, "I'm sorry, I can't. I have plans for the weekend."

He was surprised by the strength of his disappointment. "Rain check?"

Looking undecided, she nibbled on her lip before lifting soft gray eyes to his. "Um...sure," she murmured. She turned away. Then, spinning around quickly, she said a little breathlessly, "And thanks."

Rocking back on his heels, Dylan folded his arms across his chest and tilted his head to one side. "For what?"

He liked that endearing confusion on her much more than the guarded look or the haunted expression she sometimes wore when she didn't think anyone was paying attention. And he wanted to, Dylan admitted with surprise. He wanted to pay attention to her. Wanted to watch her eyes darken, to catch the quick sexy hitch of her breath, the husky laugh that burst out of her almost as though that small bubble of humor couldn't be contained. And he wanted to pay more than a little attention to that soft, full unpainted mouth.

It was as though she could read his thoughts. Her gaze flittered away from his before sliding back. A faint blush stained the high, elegant cheekbones. "For rescuing me." She laughed a little self-deprecatingly. *"Again."*

"Any time."

She took another step backward and halted, shifting awkwardly. Dylan couldn't help feeling smug that she was just as confused as he was by whatever it was growing between them, even if she *was* fighting it tooth and nail.

She fiddled with the strap of her shoulder bag and turned away, nearly colliding with a couple strolling along the sidewalk toward them. "Oops, sorry..." she said, blowing out a shaky huff of laughter. "So, I'll see you around?"

He nodded and watched her nibble on that full bottom lip, wanting her to stay so badly he could taste it—wanting to test how that lip felt against his; wanting to make it soften and open even as all those sweet curves softened against him.

"You know where to find me," he called out, watching the impatient twitch of her hips as she hurried off.

He didn't know how long he stood there with a loopy grin on his face, staring at the last place he'd seen her, until an elderly couple paused with looks of concern on their lined faces.

"You okay there, son?" the old man asked when Dylan blinked them into focus.

He lifted a hand to rub the back of his neck and wondered what the heck had just happened. He felt...*poleaxed*.

"Yeah," he sighed, rolling his shoulders to dispel the notion that he should have tried a little harder to convince her to spend the day with him. "It's…a woman."

"It always is." The septuagenarian nodded sagely. "The secret is not to try to understand them." He chuckled when his wife nudged him with her elbow. "It'll just drive you crazy."

With a wink at Dylan, the old guy moved off with his wife, leaving him to watch as he laughed and lifted their clasped hands to his lips for a sweet kiss.

Yeah. He wanted *that*. What they had. What his parents and grandparents had. The trick was to find the right woman. One who wanted *him* and not his family's money. One who wouldn't drive him crazy with the conflicting messages she sent out. Not one whose body language said one thing and whose eyes couldn't decide *what* they were saying.

Scrubbing his hands over his face, Dylan dug his hand in his pocket for his keys and headed for his Jeep, ignoring the little voice in his head that told him he was already crazy.

Crazy about a sweet little mess with big stormy eyes and a sexy smile. One who made him want to drag her into his cave and slay all her dragons. Crazy enough to want to change her mind about falling off the wagon with him.

And if that wasn't crazy enough, he thought with a shaky laugh, Dylan St. James—hotshot surgeon and heir to the St. James fortune—was feeling like a pimply-faced nerd with his first crush.

CHAPTER FIVE

A WEEK LATER Dani was awakened by the raucous sound of squabbling seagulls. Muttering about the ungodly hour on her first weekend off in over a month, she slapped a pillow over her head, determined to go back to sleep.

Five minutes later, however, she flung the pillow aside and rolled over to scowl at the ceiling. *Dammit.* Now that she was awake she'd never be able to go back to sleep. Certainly not with that racket on her deck.

She flung an arm over her eyes and sighed. Okay, so maybe the deck wasn't *hers* but since she was paying the monthly docking fees she guessed it was—temporarily, at least. Her landlord—a friend's brother—was currently living in a fancy penthouse in downtown Vancouver, because his current girlfriend hated the inconvenience of the marina and the neighborhood of floating homes.

At the time Dani had moved in she hadn't been

able to afford to be choosy. And Cole let her stay free as long as she paid the berth rates—which was *way* cheaper than any apartment within the city limits.

Now she couldn't imagine living anywhere else.

Besides, she still had a ton of student loans to pay off and she'd left her marriage with nothing. Not any of the fancy clothes Richard had paid for and none of the jewelry—except her engagement and wedding rings, which she'd sold to buy a car and pay off some of the loans. She hadn't wanted anything that would remind her of how gullible and stupid she'd been.

Her lawyer had said she was entitled to a settlement but Dani had refused. The relief of being out of that vipers' pit had been settlement enough. The fact that she still had her student loans was *her* cross to bear and no one else's. A cross she gladly carried because it meant she was free and independent.

Shoving aside memories best left in the past, she rolled to the edge of the bed, wondering what the heck was going on outside. She tossed the comforter aside and sat up, scowling as the early-morning sun—and she meant *early*—streamed through the French doors that opened onto the upper deck.

A dozen seagulls wheeled noisily in the air, while even more lifted off and then landed on the deck railing like restless spectators at a hockey match. Shoving the wild tangle of hair out of her eyes, Dani marched across the room. She'd always liked the sound of seagulls in the morning but this was ridiculous.

The instant she unlocked and pushed open the door, the air exploded with panicked squawks, beating wings and flying feathers as the birds took to the air. Stepping out, she padded over to the railing to peer down, unsurprised to see her neighbor's cat sitting statue-still, guarding something.

Axel had a habit of treating her deck like his personal hunting ground—which accounted for the regular remains of his meals. He often left gifts in front of the upper and lower French doors or, if she was careless and left a window open, either on or at the foot of her bed.

Once he'd even left a mangled lizard in her shoe. He probably thought she was a bad hunter and was providing her with food.

"Axel, shoo!"

Except for the barest tail-twitch, the black cat ignored her, his bright green eyes locked on a nearby seagull. Probably he was waiting for the birdbrain to venture closer so he could pounce.

She gave a couple of sharp claps with her hands but the bird was in a stare-down with the hefty feline, ignoring the fact that he was about to become kitty chow.

Dani took a closer look at what he was guarding and winced when she recognized a lump of downy feathers. "Dammit, Axel!" she cried, running down the stairs and across the deck.

Her sudden move caused the remaining seagulls to take flight, their raucous complaints filling the early morning. Ignoring them, she dropped to her knees and gently nudged the cat aside. He rose fluidly and head-butted her arm with rare affection, as though to say *Look what I brought you.*

"I thought I told you no more gifts?" she muttered but he turned to rub his body against her, playfully batting her hand with one heavy paw. "You're going to explode if you eat any more," she groused, gagging when she saw the pile of fuzz. "What the heck am I supposed to do with—

?" She sucked in a sharp breath. "No, no, *no*. You brought me a baby seagull? How *could* you?"

His ears twitched but he continued to wash himself, studiously ignoring her.

"Fine—ignore me," she muttered, throwing up her hands. "You're just like every other male in my life anyway."

Behind her she heard a low chuckle that had her rising and spinning around at the same time— because, one, it was coming from a neighboring floating home that was supposedly empty, two, she was standing there in an oversized T-shirt and panties and, three, it sounded awfully like—

Pain lanced through her foot as it snagged on a broken plank, throwing her off balance. She caught a fleeting glimpse of bare masculine feet, long legs encased in faded denim, a set of ripped tanned abs, sculpted pecs and rounded biceps be- fore she lost her footing and, with a shriek, made a graceless splash into the icy water behind her.

Just before the water closed over her head she saw a black streak disappearing around the side of her houseboat—of course Axel had left. Then the frigid temperature stole her thoughts as well as her breath and she gasped, getting a lungful of icy bay water. For a moment she panicked but the next thing she was breaking the surface, spluttering and coughing up water.

She tried to suck in sweet early-morning air and got a mouthful of hair instead. Treading water and shoving wet hanks out of her mouth while coughing up a lung seemed too much for her sleep-befuddled brain to handle and she found herself going under again. This time she had the presence of mind to close her mouth.

She broke the surface a second time to find those long denim-clad legs a couple of feet away...on her deck.

"You okay?"

Coughing, she peered up—*way* up—and, blinking water out of her eyes, wondered if she was seeing things or if her sleep-starved mind had conjured up the star of her most recent fantasies.

Her bleary gaze rose up those long muscular columns to the large bulge beneath a half-buttoned fly—as though he'd pulled the jeans on in a hurry—and up a happy trail to his innie, smack-dab in the middle of a taut, tanned belly.

Yum.

He dropped to his haunches. "Need a hand?"

The amusement in that deep bedroom voice

had her nipples tightening into little buds of aching need that— *Oh, wait!* That was surely because she was up to her neck in freezing water. Maybe...no, *definitely.*

Dani stared blankly up into his darkly handsome face, scarcely aware that she was gaping at him as if he'd stripped naked and was doing the hula. A little voice in her head snickered, *You wish*, and *her* voice when it emerged was a panicked squawk. "What—what are you *doing* here?"

After a long moment he jerked his head, indicating the supposedly empty houseboat behind him. The one she was meant to be keeping an eye on because its owner was somewhere in Africa.

The sliding doors were open and the deck furniture was on display. A kayak rested on a stand along with a paddle board and oars. Several colorful towels were draped over deckchairs beside a wetsuit and a white T-shirt.

She blinked at the sight of all those guy toys, wondering when the heck they'd appeared. Her voice was a shocked splutter. "You live...here... *there*?"

For a long moment he silently contemplated her

question, finally asking mildly, "Is that a problem, Dr. Stevens?"

She swallowed the news like a mouthful of ground glass. How had she not been aware of it until now?

"You're C-Cole's friend? The one who's been in Africa f-for two years?"

One dark brow rose up his forehead at the dismay she hadn't successfully hidden. With a chiding look he rose to his feet and shoved a hand through his hair, leaving the overlong strands sticking up and giving him a sexy rumpled look. She was simply *not* going to mention all that rippling anatomy displayed like eye-candy.

She gave a mental *eek* and tried to look away, because she was imagining *her* fingers running through those dark silky strands while she licked his abs right down to his open jeans.

"Why haven't I seen you?" she demanded, treading water, completely forgetting about the cold. "I mean, we share a dock. My bedroom faces out onto your deck and—"

Why hadn't she known he lived right next door? Surely she should have…*felt* something?

"I didn't know the owner was back. I've been keeping an eye on things."

His arched brow said she hadn't been doing a very good job if she hadn't noticed someone had been living there for the past few weeks.

"I've been wondering that myself," he said, studying her with amused green eyes. "The best that I can come up with is that I work days and you work nights. By the time I leave the hospital you're already at work, and when you come home I'm gone."

She thought about that for a moment and decided it made sense—especially as she'd worked the past four weekends and hadn't been home much. But that didn't mean she wanted him on her doorstep. Avoiding him at the hospital hadn't been all that difficult but with him living right next door... Well, her chances of avoiding him—and ignoring him—had just got a whole lot worse.

With his arms folded across his wide muscular chest and his legs planted apart as if he was on the deck of a rolling ship, Dylan St. James looked like a modern-day pirate...or maybe as if he belonged on the cover of a raunchy romance novel.

She hadn't realized she'd spoken out loud until his eyes filled with amusement and he tilted his head to study her. "Raunchy romance novel?" he drawled.

A tidal wave of embarrassment banished the hypothermia creeping up on her and she groaned, briefly considering drowning herself. But, since her problems couldn't be solved so easily, she swam the short distance to the deck and planted her hands on the wooden planks.

Before she could pull herself up, long masculine fingers wrapped around her wrists and hauled her out of the water. Surprise had her stumbling against him, her hands coming up against warm tanned skin to steady herself. And staying there when he sucked in a sharp breath because it was *his* fault she'd taken an early-morning swim.

She considered plastering her icy body against the front of him, then decided it would be safer— *much* safer—to beat a hasty and dignified retreat.

Before she could, he shifted his big hands to her upper arms and eased her away from him, a grin of pure masculine appreciation lighting his handsome features when he looked her over.

Realizing she looked like something Axel had

dragged in from the bay, she shoved him back and instantly missed his heat.

"Shut it," she growled, squeezing water out of her hair. "I *know* I look like a drowned rat." Her tone dared him to disagree. He lifted a hand to scratch his jaw and she knew by the amused gleam in his green eyes that he was fighting a smile.

Then his eyes slid over her and his smile became positively wicked. "Not really."

Dani looked down at herself and saw what had caused the scorching look. She gave a frantic yelp and wrapped her arms around her body to hide the way the sheer white material of her T-shirt had been suctioned against her skin like cling wrap and now exposed—well, *everything*.

Forget the wet T-shirt look—it was as if she was naked.

"Ohmigod! Stop looking!"

One dark brow rose. "Babe…" he drawled, his bedroom baritone sending heat prickling beneath her icy skin. After a moment of heated silence he shook his head and swallowed, his voice dropping to a deep rasp like the rustle of velvet against intimate skin. "I'm a man, not a saint."

Dani's body reacted as if she'd inhaled a giant

cloud of pheromones. Her head swam, her heart pounded, her ears buzzed and her skin felt as if she'd been zapped by a hundred thousand watts. She wondered if steam was rising off her skin in a cloud of vapor.

Yikes.

"This is *your* fault," she said, and scowled, attempting to pull the material away from her skin, hoping it would allow some much needed air back into her lungs—or turn the fabric opaque.

His eyes flickered and darkened even more. With her knees wobbling alarmingly, she took a step backwards, crying out as pain shot up through her foot like a bolt of lightning.

The next thing, she was yanked against a hard body.

"What's wrong? Jeez, woman, you're like ice," he cursed, his arm an iron band at her back.

"Th—that's wh-what happens when you s-swim before the sun is even up," she stuttered, wondering why her foot was throbbing like an open wound.

Her left hand slid low on his abdomen while her right gripped the waistband of his jeans, low on his hips, to help with her balance. It was only when his belly clenched beneath her icy palm that she realized exactly where her hand was. She gulped and tried to put a little distance between them but he tightened his arm and craned his neck as though he was trying to see her butt.

"What are you *doing*?" she squeaked, trying to wriggle away. "Keep your eyes *off* my backside."

"Stop squirming or I'll be seeing a lot more than damp pink panties."

She froze, her eyes wide as she recalled she was practically naked.

He dropped to his haunches, one hand sliding down her leg to her ankle. "Lift your foot."

She tried to wriggle away but his grip tightened.

"Lift."

"What? No— I— Ouch!" She sucked in a sharp breath and tried to twist around to see. "*Damn*, that hurts."

With a muttered curse, Dylan rose fluidly and swung her into his arms before she could utter a surprised squeak.

Shocked by the lack of warning—and the ease with which he'd lifted her against his chest—Dani immediately wrapped an arm around his neck and demanded, "What—what are you doing? P-put me down!"

His grunt sounded a little disgruntled, as if she'd insulted his manhood or something, and without even so much as a glance her way, he strode across the deck. Not toward *her* house-boat but his.

"Hey! Where—?" When he didn't slow down, she gasped. *"No!"*

Her eyes widened as she realized that he was going to jump the distance between the decks.

Stiffening, she yelped, "Are you *crazy*?" just as he leapt across the distance.

She tightened her stranglehold and pressed her face into his neck, giving a panicked squawk when he landed and pretended to stumble.

She rewarded the laugh rumbling through him with a punch as he strode through the open sliding doors into his sitting room. Instead of putting her down, he headed for the stairs with confident strides.

Realizing where he was going, she widened her eyes even more and stiffened again in his arms. "Dylan—"

"Relax." His growl stirred the drying curls at her temple. "I promise not to ravish you. Unless you beg me to."

"Wha—?" She whacked him again. "For God's sake, Dylan. Put me *down*."

He deposited her on the bathroom counter and reached behind him to grab a towel from heated rods. He wrapped her in its fluffy warmth.

"I need to check that foot."

Reminded of the throbbing pain, Dani pulled the thick terrycloth closer and looked down, surprised to see blood dripping onto the pristine tiles. She followed the trail across the floor and through the door into his bedroom…and beyond.

"I'm sorry." She winced apologetically. "I'll clean it up later."

His brief look said she was an idiot, and then he transferred his attention back to her foot. "You've cut yourself," he murmured, wrapping long fingers around her ankle in a way that had a shiver working its way up the back of her leg into forbidden territory.

Dani sucked in a sharp breath, and when he looked up she winced, hoping he'd mistake her shiver for pain and not—*oh, boy.*

"There's something inside…" he murmured as he probed the area gently. "I'll have to remove it." His grip gentled even as his eyes sharpened on her face. "How bad is the pain?"

She bit her lip to prevent a whimper, because it wasn't pain she was feeling. Or rather not *just* pain, she admitted, avoiding his gaze to frown down at her foot. With him so close it was hard to remember that she'd given up men. So close she could see the fine lines at the corners of his eyes and each individual eyelash. So close she got a little dizzy recalling the graphic dreams she'd had since the day she'd all but swooned at his feet.

"About a…a f-four."

His gaze traveled up her long bare legs and lingered for one heart-stopping instant at the apex of her thighs before he abruptly straightened and yanked another towel off the rail behind him, practically tossing it in her face.

Shocked by the abruptness of his action, Dani widened her eyes, her fascinated gaze locked on to the muscle twitching in his jaw. "What?" she asked, and then a little more testily, *"What?"* when his only reply was a grunt that she had no way of interpreting as he reached for her foot again.

Annoyed, she pulled away and narrowed her eyes, tempted to kick him for being annoyingly male.

"What?"

He just looked at her, his gaze heavy-lidded and unreadable. After a long silence his poet's mouth began to curl in a smile so wicked her breath backed up in her throat and sweat broke out behind her knees.

"Dylan—" *Yikes.* She'd never experienced a look that could make the backs of her knees sweat.

"I'm a little…uh…distracted." That was what she thought he murmured but it was difficult to hear anything over the thundering of her pulse.

Her fingers tightened spasmodically on the towel. "B-by what?"

For long moments he stared at her, then he stepped back and scrubbed his hands over his face. "Nothing," he said, clearly deciding a change of subject was needed. "Back to your foot. Do you have any allergies I need to know about?"

Feeling off-balance, Dani shook her head and twisted to examine the jagged cut. She pressed the area around the injury, promptly inhaling at the sharp pain.

"Stop that," he ordered, his body moving closer and blocking out the light.

She stilled, the breath catching in her throat

as she waited for his next move. Just when she thought he'd kiss her he reached up to rummage in the cabinet behind her.

"You don't know what is in there."

Her breath escaped in a silent rush that she told herself *wasn't* disappointment.

"I can fix it myself," she argued, determined to ignore the delicious masculine heat surrounding her, making her excruciatingly aware that she only had to turn her head and her mouth would brush that taut tanned skin. Her traitorous lips tingled as though she'd already done just that. "I do this stuff all the time."

He turned his head and she became distracted by the sculpted lines of his mouth, by the almost overwhelming need to press her lips to his. When he didn't move or respond, she lifted her eyes—and everything in her stilled.

His gaze was intense, searching, as though he was looking for something; searching for answers. To what? Her heart gave a little bump and every hair on her body rose—not in fear, as she'd initially thought but because it suddenly seemed as though all her life she'd been waiting for just this moment.

The air in the bathroom abruptly vanished,

sucked out by—heck, whatever *this* was that had her body simultaneously melting and tightening—leaving just the two of them in a vacuum of heat that hummed and vibrated in time to the thundering of her pulse. For long moments they stared at each other.

Dani was all but drowning in his darkening eyes as reality shifted and narrowed. It left her reeling, feeling exposed and abruptly adrift in a spiral that threatened to send her spinning into dangerous, unknown territory.

A low moan emerged from her throat, jolting her back from that dark, dangerous edge. She quickly turned away, noting that Dylan was slower to react, looking as if she'd punched him in the head.

Oh God. She knew just how that felt.

"Fortunately," he rasped, closing the cabinet door with a snap and putting a couple of feet between them, "you don't have to."

The abrupt shift from heightened sensual awareness to embarrassment was disorienting. "D-don't have to w-what?" she stammered, pretending to dry her dripping hair with one corner of the towel as she hid her hot face.

Oh God, could she be any more obvious?

"Treat it yourself," he growled.

Dani peeked up in time to see him leave the bathroom. She stared at the empty doorway, wondering what the heck had happened and terrified that she knew.

Oh God, they'd had a *moment*. A sexually charged moment. One that had left her weak and breathless and way too turned on.

Fortunately his abrupt departure was helping to clear her head. Probably from pheromone withdrawal, she thought a little hysterically and took advantage of his absence to gulp in air and will her pulse to slow down from near-coronary levels.

Maybe this wasn't such a good idea. Maybe she should just sneak out while his back was turned. Because she had good reasons for her man embargo. *Very* good reasons.

Reasons that she suddenly couldn't quite recall. Because the longer she was around Dylan, the more difficult it was to think. And therein lay the problem. He made her forget that she wasn't cut out for relationships because she didn't measure up to a man's expectations—especially in the bedroom.

She'd made herself vulnerable once before

and it had nearly ended in tragedy. But she'd managed to survive, to build a life for herself. She was stronger, sure but she didn't think she could survive another blow. Especially not from Dylan, because—she shivered—because he was the first man in years to make her feel.

If she let him.

Which meant she had to leave. *Now.* Clear out while the coast was clear.

No sooner had she made up her mind to get out of Dodge and hopped down from the counter, wincing as her foot hit the floor, than he reappeared, a mug of steaming coffee in one hand—*Oh God, she needed that*—and a medical emergency duffel slung over his shoulder.

One look at her guilty expression had a dark brow arching up his forehead. "Going somewhere?"

Flushing, she shook her head and hopped back onto the counter. She fumbled with the towel before taking the mug he offered, hugely relieved to have something to occupy her cold hands—something to hide behind as she met his hooded gaze head-on.

She hoped she was a picture of innocence but feared she looked guilty as hell. Finally he shook his head and dropped to his haunches to rummage through the duffel at his feet.

He was a big man, and his hands, broad-palmed and long-fingered, drew her fascinated gaze. She'd always been conscious of hands, of the harm they were capable of if the person they belonged to was careless. Or cruel. But she'd never been so riveted by the size or shape of a man's before.

Dylan's were big and tanned, graceful as he pulled out supplies and tossed them onto the counter. His thick wrists—well, they were thicker than hers—led to forearms that were strong with bone, muscle and sinew, the veins running beneath the skin looking both tough and fragile.

Her gaze roamed up over his powerful arm to the ball of his shoulder, admiring the play and shift of muscles beneath acres of tanned skin. Their definition was so clear that she was tempted to reach out and test the way they bunched and flexed for herself.

She could name each muscle: deltoid, pectoral, trapezius, bicep and tricep. They were common—everyone had them—but Dylan's fascinated her, drew her, because it was like looking at a work of art. Warm, satin-smooth, living art.

Drawing the towel closer, Dani frowned and thought *Holy cow—the man's lethal*. He made her want things she'd told herself were long dead. Made her want to get her hands on him when just the thought of it would have had her bolting for the door just a couple weeks ago.

"You okay?" he murmured, bent over her foot.

She gave a distracted nod and ignored the multitude of sensations bombarding her. Okay, *tried* to ignore the way her flesh buzzed and the muscles deep in her core clenched and released... then clenched spasmodically again.

Startled by the strength of the sensation—almost as if he'd actually touched her secret flesh—Dani jolted upright, her sharply indrawn breath overly loud in the silence. And when his gaze jumped to hers all she could think was, *Oh God, please let him think that was from pain and not—Oh God, not that!*

CHAPTER SIX

LOOKING UP INTO those heavily lashed gray eyes, Dylan promptly forgot everything. The expression in them—wide and a little wild—reminded him vividly of the dreams he'd battled this past week. Dreams that had left him irritable when he woke drenched in sweat, his heart beating like a runaway horse while his muscles quivered with unfulfilled lust.

Annoyed that she'd had the nerve to invade his dreams when she was so determined to avoid him during waking hours, he'd buried himself in work and deliberately avoided thinking about her. And then, just when he'd thought he might be succeeding, he'd looked up from his contemplation of the morning to see her striding across the neighboring deck, dressed in nothing but a baggy T-shirt that drooped off one shoulder and left her long, slender legs naked to mid-thigh.

At first he'd been too busy admiring the flash of those long legs to recognize her. Until her husky voice had slid across his skin like a secret wish and he'd realized his elusive neighbor was the very woman he couldn't stop thinking about.

And then, alarmed, she'd spun around and with a shocked squeak lost her balance and taken an unexpected morning dip. For one instant he'd worried that she couldn't swim but she'd surfaced looking so adorably annoyed that he hadn't been able to help laughing.

His laughter had faded when he'd hauled her out of the drink and caught a good look at the body she'd been hiding beneath her baggy scrubs. With her T-shirt clinging wetly to all those sweet curves and long slender limbs, she'd looked like any red-blooded man's wildest fantasy.

And while he'd been swallowing his tongue she'd been telling him—no, *ordering* him—to stop looking. She might as well have ordered the sun to stop shining, because he hadn't been able to. Hadn't wanted to, if he was honest. He'd liked what he'd seen—and not just a soaking wet armful of curvy contradictions.

"Dylan?"

He looked up in time to see her tongue dart out to wet her soft lips and the tension that was already setting his teeth on edge soared until the air literally crackled with it.

Blinking away the grinding lust, he inhaled, then exhaled and shifted to relax muscles he hadn't even realized had hardened. *Get a grip, man*, he ordered himself, frowning down at his hand gripping her foot. *The woman is only here because you practically shanghaied her.*

Consciously relaxing his fingers, he said, almost casually, "We're going to have to deal with this."

A tremor moved through her and he heard the click of her throat as she swallowed. She was nervous. Of him or of the sexual tension simmering between them?

Her long dark lashes fluttered against her flushed cheek and the breathy little gasp that filled the heated silence answered at least part of his question. It also shot his blood pressure to hell and it was only when she shuddered again that he realized he'd been caressing her instep with his thumb.

Shifting restlessly, she let her gaze briefly touch his before sliding away. She was trying to appear unaffected and failing miserably. It was only fair, he thought with dark amusement.

Why should he be the only one struggling to keep his mind off her long naked legs and on her injured foot?

"I…um… I thought we were?"

"I'm talking about this thing between us, Dani," he pointed out mildly.

A tiny frown marred the smooth skin between her brows. "Thing?" she asked cautiously.

Despite himself, he felt a low rumble resound through his chest. He wasn't entirely sure if it was amusement, impatience or the sound of a male animal preparing to pounce.

"For lack of a better word," he drawled, and turned his attention to disinfecting her foot, willing his hard-on to fade before she got an eyeful because he'd pulled his jeans on this morning without bothering to button them.

If she was uncomfortable discussing the chemistry that practically exploded the instant they came within twenty feet of each other, he could only imagine what the sight of his erection would do. No doubt she'd run screaming from the house to jump voluntarily into the bay, he thought with amusement.

Yep. And maybe he'd join her, because he suddenly needed an icy dip himself. It surprised him because it had been a long time since he'd felt the need for cold showers as a way to control himself around women.

Finding comfort in familiar tasks, Dylan prepared a local anesthetic and cleaned a small area of skin with an alcohol swab. He removed the needle cap with his teeth.

"You'll feel a small pinch," he murmured, immediately soothing her with his free hand when she gave an involuntary little jolt as the needle pierced her skin.

Cold fingers brushed his lips when she reached up to take the cap, sending hot, achy need spiraling downwards to his gut and digging sharp claws of need into his groin. Jeez, he was in a bad way.

It was humiliating to discover that Dylan St. James, head orthopedic reconstruction surgeon at St. Mary's, only son of Vivian and Ruben St. James and experienced man about town was being bewitched by a stormy-eyed mermaid he'd rescued from the bay. A mermaid, moreover, who'd been doing her best to run in the opposite direction ever since she'd practically fallen at his feet.

Dylan swallowed his dignity along with his

ego—which was something she appeared to deflate with annoying regularity. And if he wasn't mistaken she didn't have a clue.

It wasn't a mystery why his heart pounded and his skin itched as though something alive moved through him. What surprised him was the raw intensity of the need twisting him up inside and messing with his head.

To give himself a moment, he turned away to scrub his hands and pat them dry on a clean towel, hoping like hell she couldn't see the way they shook.

He doused them with alcohol and studied her bent head. It made him feel marginally better knowing that she wasn't as unaffected as she wanted him to believe. It was there in her parted lips, in the rapid-fire pulse at the base of her throat, and when she looked up she couldn't hide her dilated pupils or the wild flush ebbing and flowing beneath her creamy skin.

He might have put it down to embarrassment or discomfort but she couldn't hide those sexy little hitches of breath. The ones that twisted his insides like a torquing machine.

Amused at both of them, Dylan selected a pair of tweezers and got to work. He murmured an apology when she flinched and had to bite back a chuckle when she bent her head close to his and demanded, "Is it all out?" and then *"What?"* a little huffily, at the sound of frustration he made in the back of his throat.

"I'm *working* here."

She sniffed haughtily. "And how many splinters do you remove on a daily basis, Dr. Sawbones?"

"Enough to know what I'm doing, Dr. Sassy," he retorted with a chuckle. "I regularly get to remove bone splinters from bits of mangled flesh. So, yes, I've got this."

She made a skeptical noise in the back of her throat and Dylan had to restrain himself from kissing her sulky mouth. The woman was a contradiction who alternately fascinated, exasperated and amused him. She was in turn remote and cool, brisk and efficient, wary and elusive. And then there was the awkward, easily flustered woman he found incredibly appealing.

Despite the *I'm-taking-a-break-from-men* attitude, he was experienced enough to know when a woman wanted him. She either didn't trust her feelings or didn't want them. And, although it was kind of humbling to discover that the woman he was attracted to didn't want anything to do with him, he could be patient.

He could wait.

He hoped.

After satisfying himself that he'd removed all the wood slivers, Dylan irrigated and disinfected the wound before laying out the suture kit. He ignored her assurances that she didn't need stitches, shaking his head at himself when he realized he was trying to impress her with his skills.

If that didn't tell him he was losing it, nothing would.

Once he'd applied a waterproof dressing he left her muttering to herself about overkill and reached into the shower. He punched a few buttons on the console and then, before she could grasp his intentions he'd whipped off her towel, scooped her off the vanity counter and deposited her in the shower.

Her shocked gasp became a shriek of outrage as icy water rained down on her. *"Wha—what the heck are you d-doing?"* she spluttered, leaping for the opening and trying to squirm past him.

He caught her with an arm around her waist,

grinning down into her indignant face. "Just relax—it'll warm up. Just takes a few seconds."

"Relax?" she gasped, yanking him inside the cubicle and trying to use his body to shield her from the spray. "How c-can anyone relax in minus twenty d-degrees w-water?"

Trying to get a grip on her slick, squirming body, Dylan didn't feel the blast of icy water cascading over his heated flesh. Probably because all those sweet curves were sliding over him. Pulling her closer, he enjoyed the way she burrowed close and pressed her face into his throat. Although he knew it was mostly to escape the icy blast that was finally heating up. Her cool lips brushed his hot skin but his satisfaction turned into a yelp when she opened her mouth and…
bit him.

The erotic pain sent instant lust clawing at his self-restraint, digging deep and snapping the last of his control. He couldn't have stopped what happened next to save himself.

In an instant he'd pushed her up against the tiles, his body a hard weight against hers. A startled squeak had barely left her lips when he caught her mouth in a kiss so hot and hungry it rivaled the steam filling the cubicle. He took a moment to acknowledge that he should probably get the hell away from her but he hadn't ever felt this kind of desperation to touch, to taste, to feel a woman before.

Needing to get closer, he pushed one thigh between hers, at the same time thrusting his tongue into her mouth. She made little mewling sounds and slid her hands up his arms to clutch at his shoulders. He distantly comprehended that although she wasn't shoving him away, she wasn't pulling him closer either.

It was as though she'd been stunned by the heat and ferocity of his mouth. He was kind of surprised himself, since he'd never before grabbed a woman and practically inhaled her in one swoop. At the realization he abruptly gentled the kiss, corralling the wild hunger gripping him to slide his mouth temptingly along the length of hers.

This, he thought sampling the subtle flavors of her mouth, the texture of her skin, was worth the time he'd waited—was worth reining in the need pounding through him.

He tormented her with little nibbles that gradually softened her mouth and coaxed a trembling response. God, she tasted good, he thought, sliding his tongue against hers. Like deep, wet kisses on hot silky nights; like cool fresh water after being out in the African sun all day; like some delicate new flavor that burst on his tongue and left him wanting, *needing* more.

Then she moaned—a low, husky sound that had him breaking off the kiss to drop his forehead to the tiles while he struggled to get his lust under control.

What the hell was he doing? he asked himself, trying to ignore the soft, sexy curves pressed against him until not even an idea could pass between their bodies. And what must she think of him, turning all wild and savage on her?

He knew he should move but he couldn't make himself. He'd wanted the feel of her against him for too long. It made him shudder when he'd never shuddered for a woman before.

Unable to keep his hands off her, he moved back a couple of inches and curled one hand around the back of her neck. Nudging up her chin with his thumb, he rasped, "Tell me."

As though coming out of a trance, Dani blinked up at him. She looked as stunned and aroused as he felt, and so damn beautiful his chest and gut tightened.

Her mouth trembled as it opened and closed before she managed a croaked, "Wha—what?"

Dropping his gaze to her mouth, he couldn't resist swiping his thumb across that plump bottom lip. "Tell me to go, Dani," he murmured, leaning forward to nibble on that soft pillow of flesh. "And I will." He didn't want to but he would. "Say the word and I'm gone."

Dazed eyes stared into his as though she wasn't quite certain what he was asking her. "I…uh…"

Then her gaze dropped to his mouth and got stuck there for a couple of beats before she made an unconscious move, her body drawn to his in spite of herself.

Her hands relaxed on his shoulders, drawing her gaze, as though she'd only just become aware that her fingers were digging into his flesh. She gave a soft murmured apology and smoothed the marks her nails had made before trailing heat across his deltoids and pecs with her fingertips.

Her hands halted just below his nipples, then slowly spread wide, the tips of her fingers brushing each tight bud. Her tongue sneaked between her lips and he jolted, as though she'd leaned forward and swiped her tongue across his flesh.

He briefly closed his eyes and prayed for control, because the sight of those pale, elegant hands on his tanned skin and the way she was looking at him, as if he was a decadent dessert, unraveled him faster than a tumble down a flight of stairs.

It was the first time she'd touched him voluntarily and he couldn't stop his flesh from rippling—couldn't prevent the shudder that began at the nape of his neck and buried itself in the base of his spine.

The sight of those delicate hands also forced him to acknowledge just how small she was, how fragile she looked against his bulk.

And how perfectly she fitted him.

He'd never been aggressive with women, either sexually or physically, preferring to coax and charm rather than to bully. And because his instinct now was to conquer and slay he forced himself to wait and watch, while she studied the contrast between her pale hands and his tanned skin.

He wanted her to make the next move—felt *compelled* to let her make it without overt pressure from him. Because he knew instinctively that she needed to feel she had a choice, that she had control when control was an illusion for both of them.

A wild flush bloomed beneath her skin and her breath hitched in her throat before she leaned forward and pressed her mouth to his hot skin. "Stay," she murmured, her tongue emerging to flick delicately against his nipple. "I want you to stay."

He felt that teasing touch like the flick of a whip and a growl of pure need rumbled through his chest. Spearing his fingers in her wet hair, he tilted her face to his. Her lashes lifted and her gaze was dark and turbulent and sweetly seductive.

And he was lost.

Before Dani could grasp that she'd made the decision for him to stay Dylan was kissing her with such heat and hunger she felt her toes curl. She'd never had a toe-curling kiss before—one that drew her in, lifted her up on her toes and pulled a line of fire right through the center of her body, as if he was drawing out her soul along with the air in her lungs.

Her skin, exquisitely and almost painfully sensitive, prickled at the wet scrape of denim between her thighs and made her moan. She shifted restlessly, moaning inside his mouth as muscles deep in her core clenched spasmodically.

He was fully aroused, his erection a huge bulge behind his zipper, hard and insistent as it pressed into her belly. It made her hollow places clench with a need she'd never felt before. She wanted him—wanted the momentary madness that he offered, a madness that would end her four-year drought.

Tugging on his lip with her teeth, she shivered with excitement. She could finally taste him and touch him all over. She could have him thrust into her body and take care of all those pesky needs that made her so miserably aware of just what she was missing by being on the wagon. Needs she hadn't felt in more than four long years.

She could have him. And then she'd be good for another four years.

The heavy ache that settled at the apex of her thighs had her defenseless against the sensations pouring through her. *Oh God*, she thought, sliding her hands up to his solid shoulders. All she could think was *I want*.

He was everywhere—a solid heated package

of muscle and testosterone that filled her head with the warm damp smell of aroused man and her body with a sudden and pounding need. His surgeon's hands slid down her arms until they engulfed hers. Palms sliding against hers, he laced their fingers and pinned her hands to the tiles beside her head. The long, hard muscles in his thigh flexed, nearly melting her hair.

Damn, she thought faintly. He knew exactly how to make her blood heat and her mind scatter. It was there in the wicked gleam of his eyes, the sinful curve of his smile. He knew exactly where she ached, exactly where she needed him.

And he wasn't above using the knowledge to make her burn.

Her arms were pinned beside her head and the position arched her back, thrusting out her breasts like a sensual offering. She wanted him to touch her, yearned for that clever mouth to close over her aching flesh.

Frustrated by his barely there caresses, Dani shifted restlessly. She writhed against the long, thick hardness pressed to her belly, hoping to shred his control as he was shredding hers. The wanting was too painful, slicing deep and stripping away her inhibitions.

Ignoring her frustrated moans, Dylan laid a trail of kisses, sending lush sensations rolling through her as he embarked on a meandering path down her throat. He paused to suck sections of skin into his hot mouth before moving on, leaving behind a prickly, slow-spreading heat.

Despite her huffing pants, her restless movements and murmured demands, he refused to be rushed, moving from one erogenous zone to the next, ratcheting up her frustration levels until she wanted to scream.

Pinned against the wall, with solid muscle preventing her movements, Dani panted and shuddered, helpless against the onslaught of his lips and tongue and teeth. The melting eroticism left her weak, left her breath sighing between her parted lips as he thrust her into a firestorm of sensations, a world of kisses, taunting touches and a desperate burn.

Her resistance—had she really thought she had any against him?—lay in tatters, swirling down the drain along with the silky slide of water. She wanted… Her breathing quickened as she admitted to herself that she wanted *this*. Wanted *him*. Here. *Now*. Up against the wall.

She wanted fast and furious, and then she

wanted slow and deep and languorous. And then maybe she'd be able to walk away.

"Dani…" The sound of her name—deep and thrillingly rough—pulled her from her lovely sensual haze. Skin buzzing, she lifted lazy lashes to find him barely an inch away, his green eyes stark and heavy-lidded with a look she barely recognized.

"Tell me this is what you want," he ordered in a voice rough with lust.

She blinked water from her eyes and opened her mouth but nothing emerged—even though the voice inside her head was screaming, *Yes, dammit! Don't stop now!*

Arching her back, she pressed her full length against him but he held himself rigidly away from her and his voice, when it came, was laced with utter steel. "In two seconds I am going to strip you naked," he growled. "I'm going to lick every inch—and I mean *every* inch—of your body." He swooped down to score his teeth along the tendon in her neck. "And then," he murmured, sliding his tongue along the same path, "I'm going to take you to bed and rock your world so hard you're going to forget about your man embargo and fall off the wagon with me."

His words sent a shudder through her. "I…
I…" She swallowed back the embarrassing stut-
ter and gasped. "Don't…" she panted, her hands
curling into fists in his grip as muscles deep in
her core pulsed. "Don't stop."

With a low laugh and a rough curse Dylan
dragged the wet T-shirt over her head. Even before the sodden fabric hit the floor his mouth
closed over her breast with thrilling possession.
She yelped at the rough scrape of his teeth on her
nipple, arching into the wet heat of his mouth.

Sensation rolled through her like a hurricane
and something unfamiliar, hidden deep, un-
furled, stretched and tautened. For one shocking instant she thought she would climax. But
that was impossible. She'd never…couldn't…

Oh God!

As though sensing her impending release,
Dylan immediately backed off, his soothing hand
smoothing up her thigh to cup her bottom. His
fingers dug in, gripped, kneaded, the rough jerky
movements revealing his rising agitation.

He released her wrists, rasping, "God, you're
sweet," against her mouth before dropping to his
knees, chasing the goose bumps his words sent
skittering across her skin with his mouth.

Weak and dizzy, Dani clutched at him, the only solid presence in a world that dipped and tilted beneath her feet. His tongue took a fiery path between her heaving breasts and across her belly where he lingered to circle her shallow belly button before dipping beneath the narrow band of her damp panties.

Eyes glowing like emeralds in his darkly sensual face, he looked up the length of her body, making Dani's heart give a spasmodic jerk. With his mouth an inch away from her liquid heat she had a blinding epiphany that this might not be something she would recover from—that it might not be easily extinguished, easily forgotten.

Then her head dropped back against the tiles with a muffled *thunk*…and she surrendered.

From his position at her feet, Dylan took in her unconscious eroticism. With her body arched, her head thrown back and a look of intense pleasure transforming her flushed face she looked startlingly beautiful. And impossibly aroused.

He reveled in the knowledge that *he* had brought her to this point. That just a touch of his mouth—right there between her legs—would send her flying off the edge. And in that instant he felt the earth rock beneath him because despite her natural sensuality it was as though she was discovering pleasure for the first time. *With him.*

His hands shook and he forced himself to slow down. He wanted to give more—wanted to make her yearn as well as burn. He wanted to hear her cry out and then he wanted to watch her shatter.

Curling his shaking fingers in the narrow pink band at her hips, Dylan slowly drew her panties down her long legs, fighting against the need to rush. Once he'd tossed them aside he lifted one slender leg over his shoulder, gripped her thighs, and put his mouth on her—right where she was hot and wet and needy.

At the touch of his mouth Dani gave a strangled yelp and felt his lips curl against her. His mouth. *Oh God, his mouth...* Stroking, kissing, licking, nibbling every inch of her until she thought she would go up in flames.

She fisted his hair, anchoring herself even as she rocked against his mouth. "Dylan..." she gasped, her need abruptly flaming out of control, shoving her rudely to the edge before she was ready. "I… I'm going to— *Oh!*"

Pleasure burst out of her with shocking ease as he sent her hurtling off the edge. Her knees gave way and she might have slithered into a boneless heap if he hadn't risen to his feet and crushed her against him. Dazed and languid by the force of her climax, Dani could only shudder helplessly and cling.

That had been...it had been... Well, she didn't have words. Only feelings. Feelings that were still rippling through her body like aftershocks.

When she could finally feel her feet she shifted languorously, rubbing her body restlessly against his—because, as amazing as it had been, she wanted *more*. She wanted it all.

Lifting her head, she caught a flash of white teeth that was smug and sexy as hell and told her more clearly than words that he'd watched her lose it. All that masculine satisfaction had a fiery blush working its way up her neck because he'd had his mouth on her, he'd watched her…

Oh boy.

Abruptly needing to turn the tables on all that male arrogance, she reached between them to cup the large bulge straining the placket of his soaked jeans and was gratified by the sharp breath he sucked in. His flesh grew and hardened beneath her hand, sending a feminine thrill surging through her.

It was a rush to feel how her touch affected him.

"Not here," he rasped, covering her hand with his larger one and pressing hard before gently pulling away.

It was the last thing Dani wanted. "But…" she protested, curling her fingers around the buttons. "I've never had shower sex before."

He gave a rough laugh and captured her hand, lifting it to press a kiss in the center of her palm. "What do you call what just happened?"

Surprised by the gesture, she found her hand curling around the hard line of his jaw. The rasp of his beard-roughened jaw against her skin sent heat flashing right between her legs. "But you—"

"Can wait," he interrupted, stepping back to fumble at his jeans with shaking hands.

"But—"

"No condom," he panted, shoving his jeans down his legs.

And then all Dani could do was stare. Because

he was gorgeous. And—she shivered—and he'd been walking around commando...

With the water flowing over him he looked like an ancient warrior, big and bad and just a little bit dangerous as he rose, lifting his hands to wipe his face. Not knowing where to look first, because there was just so much to see and touch, Dani reached out blindly, her hand curling around the huge erection jutting between them.

He inhaled harshly, his eyes blazing heat as they caught hers. The message in them was plain: his control was hanging by a thread and she was playing a dangerous game.

Excitement shuddered through her and she tightened her grip. His eyes darkened and dropped to watch her slender fingers wrap around his bulky girth and test his heft.

It was no wonder women sighed when he walked past. Fascinated with the feel of him in her hands, Dani licked her lips. Because more than anything she wanted to taste him as he had tasted her.

Then he staggered and with a rough curse braced himself against the wall behind her. Tipping back his head, he closed his eyes. And in that moment, as Dani watched, a dull flush stained the hard slash of his cheekbones and she understood sexual power. She held it in her hands. It was there in the stark need that tightened his features.

The breath sawing from his lungs, Dylan thrust slowly into her hand before finally pulling back.

She made a sound of protest and tightened her grip. "No, I—"

Roughly turning her to face the wall, he lifted her hands to press her palms against the tiles. And just like that once again the balance shifted.

"Soon," he promised, opening his mouth against her neck to suck a patch of skin into his mouth. "I want to be deep inside you when I come."

His words made her shiver in anticipation and dread—because this was where she felt inadequate. But then he smoothed his hand from the nape of her neck to the dip in her spine and everything but the need to feel him thrusting into her body slid away.

Thinking he meant to take her from behind, Dani braced herself and waited with bated breath, groaning in disappointment and startled pleasure when his fingers dug into her scalp instead.

With slow, massaging hands he washed her

hair and then her body, making her sigh with pleasure, tremble with renewed arousal and cry out when he cupped her breasts or slid long, talented fingers between her legs.

When she was a quivering mass of unfulfilled longing he drew her from the shower and wrapped her in a large bath towel. Floating on a cloud of exquisite arousal, she felt him swing her up into his arms, feeling too wonderful to do more than hook a limp arm around his neck and sink her teeth into the ball of his shoulder.

What *was* it about him that made her want to bite him?

He deposited her gently on his bed and she roused herself briefly—only to clutch him and utter a low moan when his big, hard body followed, pressing her into the mattress with his delicious weight and inserting one hard, hair-roughened thigh between hers.

Arching her back and rocking languorously, she hummed in pleasure. It took an inordinate effort to lift her lashes. Barely an inch away, his handsome face was etched in stark lines of need, his gaze as fiercely intense as it was possessive.

"Now..." he murmured, dipping his head to nip her chin, the gentle curve between her neck and shoulder and then to swipe his tongue along her clavicle. "Now I can taste you everywhere."

Then he closed his mouth over the tip of one breast and flung her abruptly back into mindless pleasure.

Clutching the sides of his head, Dani struggled to remember why she'd thought this was a bad idea. It was wonderful, and so amazingly intense that she wanted to sink under the weight of it. Give herself to it. Let herself go. Take him with her.

But just when she felt herself sliding under his sensual spell panic, greasy and insistent, fought its way to her consciousness. Because now that they were here, on his bed, they were heading in an irrevocable direction. A direction that usually ended in disappointment.

Her heart clutched—and not in a good way. She stiffened. She had to tell him…had to stop him.

"Dylan."

CHAPTER SEVEN

TRANSFERRING HIS ATTENTION to her other breast, Dylan slid his hand up the smooth length of Dani's slender leg. He loved her little gasps and mewls, the helpless little hums of pleasure that burst from her. He'd never *needed* to hear a woman's soft sighs in response to his touch before, never craved the sight of her arching helplessly and demanding more.

Her fingers slid into his hair and clenched against his scalp but he welcomed the pain. It helped steady him as he palmed her crotch, sliding a finger between the hot glistening folds. And, God, he loved the way her body quivered and melted.

She rocked against his hand. "Dylan!" The word emerged as a strangled plea. "I… *I-don't-want-you-to-be-disappointed,*" she said on a rush.

Even as her thighs tightened around his hand something in her voice alerted him and he lifted his head and stared into her flushed face. She bit her lip and avoided his gaze, shifting restlessly beneath him as though at any second now she would bolt.

When he blinked and focused everything in him stilled. "What are you talking about?"

"I... I... I'm sorry," she stammered, blushing hotly. "I'm no good at th—this part..." Her lips trembled and she pressed them together as her eyes swam. "I'm s-sorry."

For Dylan it was a defining moment. Despite the haze of lust clouding his brain, he knew instinctively that if he handled the next few seconds badly she would retreat into herself and he'd never get another chance.

The last thing he wanted between them—especially like *this*—was the specter of another man. A man who'd made her doubt herself, draw into herself. A man who'd put that guarded look in her eyes and had her stiffening whenever Dylan touched her.

But if he wasn't patient—if he didn't show her how good it could be—it would be all over before it could begin. Before *they* could begin. More than anything Dylan wanted that beginning with her, despite her fears. And he couldn't work out why she should think she'd disappoint him when she was so lushly generous with her responses.

Eyes locked on hers, he dipped his head to place a gentle kiss on her lips. And then another. "You couldn't disappoint me, babe," he murmured, stringing damp kisses along her jaw and across the elegant cheekbone to place a brief kiss on the tip of her nose. "Trust me."

When she just looked at him, it occurred to Dylan that she didn't trust easily. She kept her emotions locked up tight and it would take a lot of patience to find the key. The guy who'd hurt her had a lot to answer for.

Gently brushing damp curls off her face, he murmured, "I won't hurt you, Dani. I couldn't. Not you."

She bit her lip, looking tempted but undecided even when it was clear she yearned to believe him. She didn't trust her own judgment. Didn't trust her own body.

He would just have to show her.

Rocking his hips gently against hers, he watched as her eyes darkened and her lashes fluttered as his shaft slid against her tender flesh. Then she sighed, a sound of such sensuality that he wanted to catch it in his mouth before it escaped.

Her eyes dropped to his mouth and she lifted a hand to trace a fingertip along the line of his bottom lip. Giving in to the urge, he parted his lips and drew her finger into his mouth.

"Just relax and let me make it good."

"It's just this," she murmured, sliding her finger free to cup his face, her palm warm and soft against his rough cheek. "This is all I can offer. Once. Here with you."

Covering her hand with his, he turned to press his lips against the soft skin of her wrist. He wanted to argue because he had a bad feeling that once wouldn't be enough—wouldn't be *nearly* enough.

"Yeah…" he rasped, pressing his hips closer and nudging her with his erection. "And then we'll do it again and again…until we're done."

Wild color rushed into her face and she snorted. "I meant—"

"I know," he promised with a wicked grin. "I know exactly what you meant. But just so you know," he added, his gaze and his voice softening, "you couldn't disappoint me if you tried."

And then, because he had only one chance to

convince her that once would never be enough, Dylan set his mind to seducing her. Despite his own impatience, the pounding of his blood, he began with hot drugging kisses that swept away her tension and replaced it with another kind of tension. Until she was moaning and rocking into his teasing touches with an eagerness he'd never encountered.

God, she was sweet. And she'd thought she wasn't enough...

He ruthlessly overwhelmed her with sensation until she was writhing beneath him, teetering on the edge of another orgasm as she begged him to take her. And when he finally rolled a condom down the length of his shaft, captured her mouth and thrust into her body, he felt as though he'd come home.

She was tight, incredibly tight, and he had to resist the urge to bury himself deep. But the moment he breeched her entrance her body clamped down on his invasion like a velvet vice.

Pausing to tangle his hands in her damp hair, Dylan shuddered and breathed through his lust. He gritted his teeth and pressed in another inch, scattering desperate little kisses down her neck and across her shoulder to her breast.

"Relax," he rasped, his voice strained as he carefully drew back an inch, then eased forward again.

He smoothed his palm down her thigh to her knee, enjoying the feel of the long slender muscles flexing beneath silky skin. Curling his hand beneath her knee, he lifted her leg to ease his entrance, watching each expression as it flittered across her beautiful face.

She might lock down her emotions, he thought, gritting his teeth but she couldn't keep her thoughts from showing on her face. It fascinated him to see discomfort at war with desire, excitement and a growing sensual impatience.

She shifted restlessly beneath him as he smoothed damp hair off her forehead with shaking fingers. "You okay?"

God. A woman had never made him shake before.

"I'm f-fine," she gasped, a flush rushing across her chest and up her neck into her face. Clutching at his shoulders, she wrapped her legs around him and arched up into his embrace. "Oh God, it feels so...*good.*"

And, with his gaze locked on hers, Dylan pulled back again and slowly thrust in deep, drawing a low moan of pleasure from her throat. Muscles burning with effort and eyes fierce, he captured her hands and laced their fingers tightly together.

"Keep your eyes on mine, babe," he huffed out with effort. "And hang on. I'm going to rock your world."

I'm going to rock your world.

Dani bit her lip as heat gathered between her legs and spread across her belly. Her foundations were already shuddering and she wondered if she would survive this sensual attack.

With him filling her completely, stretching her inner muscles, she could almost believe that she wouldn't disappoint him. Almost believe that she could be what he needed, what she desperately wanted to be. For him.

But that wasn't going to happen, she admitted with regret, because she knew from experience that once a guy got to this point he lost the plot along with his control and she always needed more time. More time to get into the mood, to strain for that moment of glory.

Dylan hadn't wanted to listen, so all she could do now was try to make it as good for him as

possible and hope he didn't notice her lack of...
well, *finishing.*

He was the first man in a long while to make
her feel like a woman—the first man to make
her feel as though this amazing feeling was possible, that she could let herself go long enough
to be swept away. It was an amazing feeling. Almost as amazing as the feel of him inside her,
surrounding her, the scent of him in her lungs
as he moved over her, thrusting deep over and
over and over.

Her inner muscles quivered. Heat was building,
spreading. *Oh God, had it ever felt this good?*

Keeping his strokes ruthlessly slow and deep,
Dylan stared into her eyes until the thread deep
inside her belly drew tight. She trembled, finding the way he looked at her more intimate than
his possession. She wanted to look away, to shut
her eyes and lose herself in physical sensation.
Maybe then she could—

She jolted when he nipped at her lip. "Stay with
me," he growled, and her eyes flew open to that
fiercely intense gaze as he thrust long and hard
and deep.

She rocked against him more frantically.
"Please..." she gasped, clutching at him, des-

perate to hang on to the only stable thing in her wildly spinning world.

His slick muscles rippled beneath her fingers, oiled steel straining with the effort to keep his rhythm slow and deep as he ruthlessly drove her toward something as tantalizing as it was elusive.

"Please…" she sobbed again, unsure whether she was asking him to stop or to take his pleasure, because she wouldn't…*couldn't* come. Not like this.

Ignoring her pleas, Dylan kept his eyes on hers, kept her hovering on the edge as that thread tightened, building…building…until one hard downward thrust drew her completely under.

Her body arched up as she came, his name a hoarse cry of stunned pleasure bursting from her lips. She clung to him, the walls of her body clenching and pulsing around him as his thrusts increased in tempo and strength, sweeping her away into another helpless orgasm even more intense than the first.

Breath rasping like bellows, he finally slammed into her one last time, driving her up the bed with the force of his own climax. His muscles turned to stone and his eyes were a fierce green blaze in his tight face. Then the breath whooshed from his lungs as though he'd slammed into a wall, and he threw back his head and emptied himself into her.

Finally he gave a rough groan and collapsed over her, buried his face in her neck, his arms bands of iron as he held her to him. And all Dani could do was cling on and drift on a cloud of sensual delight.

She might have been stunned by what had happened if she'd been able to think. Locked to him, around him, her body pulsing with little aftershocks, all she could do was feel.

And she felt fantastic—so fantastic that all she could think of was that she wanted to hold it to her for just a little while longer.

She didn't know how long they lay like that but when her heart-rate slowed to just under stroke level she became aware that she was wrapped around him as though she was terrified he would vanish.

Embarrassed to be caught clinging, she quickly released him and tried to push him off.

Lost in the hazy aftermath of spectacular sex, Dylan felt her pulling away and instantly tightened his arms. He didn't want to move; he wanted to keep them joined, keep this incredible feeling just a little longer.

He flexed his hips and smiled at the odd little sound she made in the back of her throat—kind of a mix between a squeak and a wheeze as her body rippled around his shaft.

And then she gave another little shove.

Groaning, Dylan managed to get his elbows under him. He didn't want to move. He liked being this close to her, their bodies still intimately joined. He liked the feeling of their sweat-slicked skin fused together and the way their combined scent filled the air.

He looked at her. Really looked. And he was pleased to see the rosy glow flushing her skin even as she evaded his gaze. He continued to study her, smug in the knowledge that he'd made her come not once but twice. All while buried so deep inside her he hadn't known where he ended and she began.

His grin widened. So much for disappointing him.

The rosy glow deepened. "Stop that," she muttered, giving him another little shove.

"Stop…?" He chuckled, dipping his head to taste the pulse thundering at the base of her throat. Her muscles quivered as he slid a broad palm down her back to the base of her spine, where he pressed, keeping them connected.

It was when he rolled them over that he realized why he'd never felt anything so good.

The condom had broken.

The knowledge was like an icy slap in the face.

As carefully as he could, he lifted her off him and slid off the bed, heading for the bathroom as reality hit him like a blow to the head. No wonder sex had been better with her than with any other woman. No wonder being inside her had felt like being wrapped in hot wet silk.

His breath escaped in a whoosh but this time he really *had* hit a brick wall… Because right now his little swimmers were heading for Ground Zero.

Cursing, he quickly disposed of the condom and cleaned up before grabbing the edge of the counter to steady himself. He closed his eyes and dropped his head between his shoulders as reality washed over him. For the first time in twenty years he was facing the possibility of an unplanned pregnancy and…

Abruptly he pushed himself upright and caught sight of his reflection. *Hell.* He looked like hell.

He froze and took another look. Actually, no, he decided, he looked as if he'd just had the most spectacular sex of his life.

Cursing again, he turned and grabbed a pair of jeans that were draped over the laundry basket, pulling them on with jerky movements. In seconds he was yanking at the zipper with unsteady hands, telling himself that they would face it when—*if*—it happened.

He took a moment to splash his face with cold water and then he caught movement out of the corner of his eye. Face dripping, he turned to see her standing a couple of feet from the deck doors, wrapped in his sheet, her eyes wide and distressed in her pale face.

He grabbed a towel and dragged it over his face to give himself a minute. It wouldn't do to lose it now—not with that look on her face.

When he looked again she was still exactly as she'd been, frozen like a deer scenting danger.

With the morning light pouring in through the doors she looked like a young Eve, wildly beautiful and thoroughly ravished. Her pale neck and shoulders rose above the sheet, and even from here he could see the reddened patches of whisker burn and hickeys beginning to darken her creamy skin.

She was poised to run, and something…*something* in her eyes…warned him to be careful how he handled the next few minutes—warned him that she was bracing herself for… What? Movement? Violence? Anger?

Despite his inner turmoil, the panic in her eyes made him feel sick inside—because a woman didn't look like that for no reason. It steadied him as nothing else could have.

Tossing the towel aside, Dylan took a step—and stilled when her eyes widened and she stumbled back. For a long tense moment he watched her nibble nervously on her lip, swallowing the words that sprang to his lips.

"I told you, I'm no good at…at that." She gulped, struggling for composure as she went red, then white, then red again. "I tried to tell you but—"

"I'm not *disappointed*, Dani," he interrupted, aghast that she could think so.

But clearly she did, because the wariness was back and she looked ready to bolt at the first move from him.

Sucking in a steadying breath, he said quietly, "You felt it as much as I did."

Her posture relaxed slightly but her eyes remained locked warily on him, as though waiting for him to attack. *What the hell?*

He shoved impatient fingers through his hair, furious with himself for the fine tremor in them. Dammit, if there was ever a time he needed control it was now. Unfortunately it felt as though she'd wrested his control from him with that first look into her soft gray eyes.

"Tell me you're on the pill."

A quick frown drew her brows together. "What?"

"Birth control," he rasped, cursing himself when she flinched. Exhaling carefully, he said more quietly, "The condom broke."

For long moments she stared at him, confusion swirling in that stormy gray gaze. Then abruptly her eyes cleared, her brows drawing together as his meaning became clear.

Her breath escaped in a quiet whoosh. "Oh."

When she looked neither pleased nor distressed by the news, it was up to Dylan to repeat, "*Are* you?" his fingers tightening painfully on the door frame.

Expression carefully neutral, she said, "No,"— so softly he almost didn't hear it above the pounding of his heart.

He let out a soft curse, his fingers white-knuckling the doorjamb. "So you could get pregnant?"

Her gaze instantly shuttering, she turned and moved to the open deck doors, drawing Dylan's gaze from the long, elegant line of her naked back to the twin dimples at the base of her spine.

The urge to drop to his knees and put his lips there rattled him and he crossed the carpet on silent feet, telling himself it was to keep her from bolting down the stairs.

"No, I can't," she said in a low voice when he came to a stop behind her.

"How can you be so sure?" He wanted to put his hands on her, to soothe the tension pumping from her in almost visible waves.

She gave a ragged laugh and lifted shaking fingers to shove wild, tousled curls off her face. "Because it's impossible."

Studying her delicate profile, the tense set of her shoulders, Dylan thought back to when she'd been flushed and sated. He wished he could turn the clock back five minutes.

"What do you mean, 'impossible'?"

For long moments she didn't speak, and then her jaw hardened. She turned to lean back against the open French door and her gaze was coolly amused. "I mean I have Asherman's syndrome," she drawled. "So I guess that lets you off a very unpleasant hook, Dr. St. James."

Ignoring the subtle bite in her tone, Dylan's eyes narrowed, dropped to her belly where he'd seen and traced those thin silvery scars with his tongue. "Asherman's?"

"I had an accident…years ago," she said with careful neutrality, as though they were discussing a patient. But Dylan caught the convulsive movement of her throat as she swallowed. "A bad one."

Her fingers tightened almost imperceptibly as she dragged the sheet closer. As though to protect herself from the words, from *him*.

"There…um…there was a lot of internal scarring and—" Her delicate brows drew together and she hitched a bare shoulder, the movement jerky and filled with a roiling tension. "The gynecologist said my chances of ever conceiving were negligible." She spun away and sent him a mocking glance over her shoulder. "So you see why this is just a one-time thing?" She looked away. "Men want certain…things. Things I can't give them."

Dylan took the step that separated them and wrapped his arms around her resistant body, drawing her back against his chest. She didn't pull away but stood rigidly in his embrace, tension vibrating through her like a tuning fork.

"You have no idea what I want, Dani," he said deeply, pressing a kiss to her naked shoulder. "But I think we can safely say that I'd be an idiot if I didn't want more of what just happened."

She jerked her shoulder irritably. "That's just *sex*, Dylan," she scoffed, and he fought not to feel offended by her quick dismissal of what had been the best sex of his life.

"Pretty spectacular sex," he reminded her with a trace of humor, smug satisfaction rising in him when she gave a helpless little shiver at the reminder.

Damn, he wanted her again, he admitted silently. She was soft and warm and, despite the driving need to toss her back onto that bed and remind her just how spectacular it had been, more than anything he wanted her trust. He wanted her to relax, to laugh. He wanted her to open herself to him, to turn to *him* when demons kept her awake at night.

Discovering a yearning inside him for all that left him reeling. They'd only just met, he told himself. It would be insane to think this was anything more than what it was: two sexually compatible people having spectacular sex.

Dylan tightened his arms and inhaled the scent of warm, sexy woman. If this was all she would take from him, he decided, then he'd focus on giving it to her. *For now.*

He continued to nuzzle her neck until his patience was rewarded. Her body slowly relaxed against him, although she didn't turn and she didn't try to touch him. Relieved, he brushed a kiss against the tender curve between her neck and shoulder.

Beneath the scent of his soap he could smell both of them. He could smell a unique fragrance that was all her, and the discovery made him want to imprint his scent on her as much as he feared hers was imprinted on him.

Hungry for more, he licked her skin, enjoying the taste of warm freshness overlaid with the faint saltiness of exertion.

A shiver moved through her. She tilted her

head to one side to give him more room to run his mouth up to nibble on the tender skin beneath her ear. Mouth curving against her skin, he buried his face in the soft cloud of dark curls, tenderly running his hands up and down her arms, warming her chilled skin.

Finally she gave a ragged sigh and turned to him, her hands leaving a line of fire across his pecs and down his abdomen. She brushed her mouth across his nipple, small white teeth emerging to nip at the tight bud.

He shuddered. The feel of her mouth on him ratcheted up his hunger until he felt as if he hadn't recently experienced that explosive, bone-melting orgasm. And, with his legs threatening to buckle, he swung her into his arms, determined this time to taste the long elegant line of her spine down to those sexy little dimples. He would taste her secret places and watch her face as he thrust into her body.

He wanted to be staring into her soul when she shattered.

It was just sex, Dani told herself for the hundredth time. Incredible, mind-blowing sex it was true but just sex. And now it was over. She could go back to being on the wagon and enjoy being alone.

And maybe if she repeated that to herself enough she might begin to believe it. She might feel amazingly alive for the first time in her life—alive, consumed and possessed—but that didn't mean he wanted anything more than she did.

He lived in his world; she lived in hers.

But if it was difficult to forget the incredible sex—an amazing first for her—what had come after was even harder. He'd teased and cajoled her to spend the day with him, and before she knew it, it was two on Monday morning and she was limp as a rag doll from yet another mind-blowing orgasm.

She'd lost track of how many she'd had—a miracle in itself, considering she'd believed herself incapable. As she'd lain there, boneless and mindless, it had dawned on her that anything that came after would be anti-climactic.

He'd been wonderful, so sexy and romantic, and he'd made her *laugh*. It was the first time anyone had made her laugh as well as sigh while he was buried deep inside her body.

Nothing had ever come close to this intense

feeling of rightness, and she was afraid that if she stayed she would start thinking that it was more than just sex. Because, despite her determination to keep it simple, she'd found herself sharing stuff about her family, about growing up geeky and nerdy and largely ignored by boys because she was shy and smart.

When he'd said *he* wouldn't have ignored her, she'd scoffed. "Girls like me are invisible to boys like you."

"Boys like me are idiots," he'd said, and when she'd rolled her eyes he'd gone on to tell her about why he'd needed to get away after losing his grandfather and a close childhood friend so close together. Working aboard the Mercy Ship, he'd admitted, had opened his eyes to the plight of children in war-torn countries and he was determined to do something to help.

How could she not be swept away when he was so darn likeable? Not just wickedly funny but dry and insightful. And then there was that incredibly sweet streak.

He'd likely be horrified that she thought him sweet but what else could she think when a man made time for a lonely neighbor on the houseboat moored at the next berth? Or answered the endless questions Hilda Frauenbach peppered him with about poisons found in Africa and whether the African pygmy was hostile?

She'd found herself watching, waiting for the mask to crack and the impatience to show but it hadn't. Either he was better at hiding his emotions than most people, or he really was what he seemed.

How did a woman resist a man who was amazingly patient and affectionate outside of bed and so thrillingly impatient in it? A man who spoke of his family in a way that told her of the deep love and respect he had for them. A man who didn't ridicule her opinions or force his on her. A man who respected her reticence even as he tempted her to throw caution to the wind.

He'd told her about the woman he'd met on the Mercy Ship and how she'd tried to pass off another man's baby as his, laughing when Dani expressed her outrage.

"I'm lucky," he'd said, smiling sleepily down at her. "If I hadn't overheard Simone bragging to that nurse I might not have been there to rescue you from that killer puddle."

She'd rolled her eyes but her belly had jittered nervously at the implication that he was glad he'd been there that night when she didn't know *how* she felt. She'd told him how she'd met Richard and hinted at bits of her marriage but she couldn't—wouldn't *ever*—tell him about the bad stuff because it was her shameful secret.

And if something inside her had trembled in envy when he'd talked about wanting the kind of relationship his parents and grandparents had, Dani ignored it and allowed him to sweep her up into a fantasy of shared laughter, hot glances and mind-blowing sex.

With him wrapped around her, his deep, even breathing disturbing tendrils of damp hair at her temple, she tried to ignore the panic that had crept up on her until she couldn't breathe.

Old insecurities came flooding back, until it was all she could do not to run screaming into the night. She waited until his hold loosened and then she slid quietly away. Like a memory.

Because that was all their weekend could ever be: a time out of time. She was back on the wagon and they were back to being just neighbors and colleagues.

Yep. Neighbors and colleagues. Exactly as it was supposed to be.

Now all she had to do was convince herself that

was what she wanted. She was back on the wagon and… Well, memories—the kind they'd made these past two days—were better than regrets.

CHAPTER EIGHT

DYLAN HADN'T BEEN surprised when he'd awakened on Monday morning to find himself alone and the bed beside him cold.

For just a moment he'd thought he'd imagined the whole weekend. Then he told himself he'd go and find her in the kitchen, brewing coffee and burning eggs. She'd be dressed in nothing but his T-shirt, looking adorably rumpled as she frowned down at the scrambled mess she'd made of breakfast.

He'd pull her back against his chest and slide his hands beneath the baggy shirt where he'd find warm, supple curves and soft, slender woman. Then he'd kiss her neck and inhale the fragrance of heated feminine skin. At his touch she'd give a delicious shiver, before turning to lift her mouth to his. Then he'd kiss her, lift her onto the counter and press his morning erection between her open thighs.

But even as the image appeared he knew without being told that the houseboat was empty of her. Empty and quiet. And the prospect of long, languid kisses and lazy morning sex became nothing but a fantasy.

He'd think their whole *weekend* nothing but a fantasy if not for the scent of her on his sheets—and on his skin, he thought, sniffing his arm. She'd burrowed beneath it, dug sharp claws into his gut and chest and left without a thought.

Anger moved through him as it dawned on him just how empty his life was when he'd thought himself content. He had an amazing family who loved him and a career on the fast track. His professional life was busy and fulfilling and—he cursed and shoved a shaky hand through his hair—his personal life sucked.

Damn. He should have known yesterday, when she'd become more and more distant, that she'd been subtly pulling away even as he'd tried to bind her more tightly to him—to seduce her with pieces of his life, with laughter over his fumbled ten-year-old attempts at being a cool man about town and shared intimacies.

Perhaps that had been what had spooked her. Dani was afraid of being truly intimate.

With him? Or with any man?

Not the intimacy of sex, he mused, stomping around his houseboat in a rare flash of masculine pique. Once she'd overcome her initial fear of disappointing him she'd been generous and wildly passionate. But she'd shared very little of her emotions or the real reason her marriage had failed. And it was there he knew he would find the answers to the mystery that was Danielle Stevens.

Her ex had certainly done a number on her, he thought with growing anger. He'd made her believe she wasn't good enough, that she had little to offer a man. He'd all but stripped a vibrant, generous woman of her confidence in her own femininity and convinced her that she was better off alone.

Dylan had grown up in a house full of women. He didn't consider himself a particularly sensitive man—he had too much testosterone for that—but he couldn't understand the need some men had to break a woman down. Strip her of everything that made her such a delightful bundle of contradictions.

He wasn't stupid. He knew such men existed. But he'd never understood them. Never understood their need to belittle, to grind away at someone's confidence in themselves.

And Dani...? He recalled the sound of her laughter and the way it had made him feel the first time it had bubbled from her throat. That irrepressible gurgle of mirth had made him feel ten feet tall, because *he'd* been the one to draw it out of her.

Then she'd slipped away without a word, and left him feeling as though she'd taken all the sunshine, all the warmth with her. It made him angry. More with himself because he'd slipped under her spell as easily as she'd burrowed beneath his skin.

In one weekend, damn it.

But Dylan wasn't a St. James for nothing. He wasn't about to give up and he'd be damned if he'd allow anyone to come between him and the woman he wanted. Even the woman herself. And if he wanted Danielle Stevens, in his bed and in his life, more than he'd ever wanted anything— *any woman*—before, all he had to do was convince her to fall off the wagon with him again.

Piece of cake.

If only he could get her to answer her phone or return his damn messages.

* * *

Dani had taken to hiding in the ER supply room. She knew it was a cowardly thing to do but she couldn't face Dylan until she had her feelings firmly locked down or people would take one look at her and know that she'd had wild, uninhibited sex with the hot-shot surgeon.

Heat swept through her body and burned in her cheeks. *Oh boy.* If just the memory had her sweating in indecent places, she could imagine what would happen if she found herself face to face with him in company.

She'd never met a man who could so easily make her forget that she had good reason to avoid relationships. Or one who refused to acknowledge their very temporary arrangement.

Besides, he had dozens of women calling him, "accidentally" bumping into him wherever he went—even when she'd been with him, for heck's sake. Granted, he hadn't seemed to notice or care, she recalled with a secret thrill. Instead he'd focused all his attention on her, which made him either very well brought up or very, very sneaky. What woman *wouldn't* find all that attention flattering and just a little bit intoxicating?

She certainly had.

But it would be really stupid to think it meant anything more—that he wanted anything more. And Dani had already used up her quota of stupid for one lifetime. She couldn't—*wouldn't*—let herself forget that it hadn't meant anything more than a weekend of fun.

So she'd ignored his calls and texts, hoping he'd get the message, give up and spare her the humiliation when he eventually moved on. Because that was what guys like him did. They moved on.

Unfortunately her heart and her body didn't get the message, and kept insisting that she answer his calls. Fortunately she'd been swamped with work whenever he came around and when she hadn't been she'd managed quite neatly to avoid him.

Even as she'd congratulated herself for handling the weekend with such modern sophistication she'd struggled with the emotional fall-out. She was, she discovered, entirely unsuited for one-night stands—one-weekend stands. What she *was* suited for, however, didn't matter, because she'd been the one to insist on a one-time thing and she always tried to keep her word.

Besides, she reminded herself, she had very

little to offer a man like Dylan, and thinking that she might be falling for him was dangerous and stupid.

So stupid that she was hiding out in the supply room, trying to convince herself that everything was back to normal. She rolled her eyes. If you could call sneaking in and out of her own home the past ten days normal. Or letting his calls go to voicemail. She couldn't even think how his number had got onto her phone.

She was back on the wagon, she told herself firmly, back to living like a nun and loving every minute of it. *Really.* She could do whatever she liked, whenever she liked, and there was no one to distract her from doing it. Things like her laundry. Things like cleaning out the refrigerator, giving herself a homemade facial or scrubbing her bathroom to within an inch of its life... for the third time in less than two weeks.

And she'd spent a delightful, if unplanned weekend with her parents on Vancouver Island, telling herself that she wasn't running away. She wasn't falling for him and she wasn't avoiding him.

The only reason she hadn't deleted his voice messages was because she'd been too busy. And if she listened again to the sound of his voice, especially late at night, it wasn't because she was reliving the weekend like a giddy adolescent with her first crush.

It *certainly* wasn't because she was crushing on Dylan St. James just like every other woman at St. Mary's. That would be beyond embarrassing. Not to mention really stupid. She was a mature, professional physician who could have a brief, steamy affair with a hot guy without getting her emotions or her heart involved.

That particular organ had been killed off by her marriage and it wasn't likely ever to be resuscitated. And certainly not for a pair of wicked green eyes, a deep bedroom voice that slid into her secret places and a mouth that could tempt an angel to fall from grace.

Nope. Nuh-uh. Not likely.

Besides, how could an intelligent woman possibly fall for a man she'd known less than two months? It was impossible—not to mention ridiculous. Despite all signs to the contrary and despite her friends' and colleagues' concern at her distraction.

An ER doctor couldn't afford to be distracted, even during the graveyard shift on a night so slow that she'd checked her phone no less than forty-six times—apparently Amy had counted—for new messages, before escaping to the storeroom.

But, then again, Dylan hadn't called or texted her for three days.

Fine, she admitted, frowning at the packages of wet dressings on the shelf. Three days, seventeen hours and fifty-two minutes. Clearly he'd moved on. *The jerk*.

Pressing a hand to her queasy stomach, she rearranged the packages and counted them—for the third or was it the fourth time? She was muttering to herself when she heard the door open and close. Thinking that Amy—the woman gave *determined* and *obstinate* a bad name—had resorted to cornering her there, Dani sighed.

"Amy, I'm *fine*," she growled with extreme exasperation, glad she was hidden amongst the rows of shelving. "For the ten millionth time, *I am fine*. I'm a little under the weather but I do not have any dreadful disease that requires a visit to a physician." She sucked in an irritated breath. "I *don't* have a brain tumor and I am *not* pining away for any Y-chromosome with hot green eyes *and a sexy butt*!"

She paused in her rant to scowl at the tablet she was checking against the supplies. She ground her teeth together when she caught movement out the corner of her eye.

"You need to get laid," she said irascibly, turning to face Amy. "Focus on your own sex life and not— *Dylan!*"

To say she was surprised to see him propped up against the end of the row of shelves in his scrubs was an understatement.

She gave a shocked shriek and tumbled backward, her scrabbling fingers missing the wooden shelving completely and sweeping several boxes of syringes and surgical gloves onto the floor, along with half the neatly arranged wet dressing packages.

She slapped the hand clutching the tablet against her tachycardic heart and gasped. "What the—? You scared me!"

He folded his arms across his wide chest—and she *wasn't* noticing the way his biceps, triceps and all those flexor and extensor muscles bulged at the movement. She *wasn't* recalling every detail of their weekend together.

His unreadable eyes studied the way she was clutching the tablet to her chest as though it could protect her from him. After what seemed like a millennium his eyes took on a twinkle and his mouth began to twitch. "You think I have a sexy ass?"

"Wha—? *No.* Yes... I mean... *That's* what you got from all that?"

"No." He chuckled, pushing away from the shelving. "I also got that you've been pining for my wicked green eyes. But I agree about needing to get laid. In fact—"

She hastily backed up a half-dozen steps, her eyes widening as he kept coming. "Don't flatter yourself... What are you *doing*?" she yelped when he backed her against the wall and dipped his head to nip her throat then soothe the hurt with his tongue.

"You can't tell?" His drawl was a rough growl of temptation against her flesh and in two seconds she was breathing hard—from annoyance, she told herself. Her knees *weren't* wobbling and that *wasn't* her moaning.

Oh God, it was. How embarrassing!

Her hands clutched at him—when had she reached out?—and she angled her head to one side so he could slide his lips up to the soft spot beneath her ear.

She shivered. "Dylan?"

"Mmm…?" He hummed against her ear, sending an armada of goose bumps sailing across her flesh.

Ooh. Not good…or maybe *too* good.

"What…what are you doing?" she squeaked as he nipped her earlobe.

"I'm saying hello…and punishing you."

Her nipples peaked and her breasts tightened. "What?" she gasped, trying to push him away and finding to her horror that she couldn't. Her fingers had curled into his shirt and they were holding on. "Why?"

"For ignoring me the past ten days," he murmured taking a little bite out of her lip. "Ten days, seventeen hours and thirty-eight minutes."

"But we…you… I…" Disbelief moved through her. *He'd also been counting?*

He ignored her breathy protest. "For leaving me alone in my bed," he murmured against the corner of her mouth when her breath escaped in a shuddery gasp. "For turning my bed into a cold, barren wasteland."

"But I…you…we—"

"You already said that." He chuckled softly, sliding his hands beneath her scrubs top and palming her breasts, satisfaction lighting his dark eyes when she moaned. "Only the other way round."

"I…um…" She licked her lips and dug her fingers into his biceps, her body already arching into his big warm hands.

How was she supposed to talk, let alone think when he was brushing his thumbs over her aching nipples?

"I'm back on the wagon," she managed to get out on a rush of air, before he rendered her speechless.

He paused and lifted his head from where he'd been tasting the hollow in her throat—right where her pulse flopped like a fish out of water. His eyes were dark and heavy with lust as they stared into hers.

"I missed you," he murmured, tugging her closer. "I didn't expect to miss you so much."

Terrified of what he might see there—the little smile she couldn't quite prevent at his words—Dani quickly looked down to see his hands moving beneath her top, sliding away from her breasts.

She bit her lip against the automatic protest that rose but instead of removing his hands he was smoothing them around her back and sliding them beneath the elastic waist of her scrubs pants—and *her panties*—to cup her bottom as he pressed one hard thigh between hers.

"Is that why you're undressing me?" she squeaked breathlessly.

"I like *your* bottom too," he whispered, dragging his lips across her cheekbone to her ear. "It's soft and sexy and it fits perfectly in my hands."

His fingers clenched and unclenched on her bottom until she mewled at the heat gathering between her legs. "Are you saying I have a…a big *butt*?" She gasped, blinking rapidly to clear the lustful haze from her brain.

He paused in the process of swiping his tongue across her clavicle before moving back an inch so he could stare down into her face. At her aroused, outraged expression, he chuckled. "Seriously?" His fingers clenched again, drawing a little squeak from her throat. "Here I am, waxing lyrical about how I feel about your body, and all you can think is that I mean your butt is big?"

"You have big hands," she pointed out.

"All the better to do this…" he murmured wickedly, and slid two fingers into her.

The surprise invasion drew a shocked squeak from her lips that he captured with his mouth.

"Shh…" he warned against her lips. "We don't want anyone storming in here thinking you're being ravished…or do we?"

Dani shook her head, too far gone to object to what she could only think of as an ambush—if she'd been able to think, that was.

She wasn't.

Every thought save the one telling her she needed to remain standing slipped away under the onslaught of his hot, hungry kiss and the long, flexible fingers between her legs.

His mouth caught her shocked and aroused moan and all she could do was clutch at him and move against his fingers. Just before her eyes rolled back in her head he ended the kiss and removed his hand, leaving her weak-kneed, gasping for breath and on a very fine edge.

Her legs gave way and the next thing she knew she was sprawled in his lap while he held her against him, his arms two bands of iron across her back. She sucked in ragged breaths redolent of warm, delicious man and realized her face was pressed against his throat. After a couple of beats she opened her mouth—to say what, she had no idea—but all that emerged was a death rattle.

"You okay?" Dylan growled, his breath stirring the soft curls at her temple.

"I think…" she gasped "…I th—think someone stole my b-bones."

"That would be me."

He sounded way too smug for Dani's liking but she was too stunned by the force—and speed—with which he'd whipped her up to object.

Sighing, she snuggled closer and licked his throat. "I want them back."

"Not yet."

It took her a full minute to realize that she was draped over him like a tablecloth in the supply room, where anyone might find them. It would take about five minutes for the gossip to reach Oncology, which was over in the East Wing.

The thought was enough for her to recover her bones, if not her mind.

"Ohmigod!" She gasped, scrambling to her feet in horror. "Are you *insane*? I can't believe you just did that. I can't believe I *let* you do that."

"I didn't do anything…yet," Dylan drawled, leaning back against the wall, a satisfied grin pulling at his mouth.

"Stop that," she ordered as she tried to find her balance. "I don't know what you're looking so smug about. It's not like you…" She gestured to the erection tenting his scrubs pants and blushed. "Dealt with *that*," she ended on a half-hysterical laugh.

"You going to take care of it for me?"

"No!" She gasped again, laughter bubbling up from a place deep in her chest. "It serves you right for ambushing me when I'm so busy."

He looked at the supplies scattered across the floor. "Busy, huh?"

She smoothed her hair off her face with shaking hands and turned away to begin collecting boxes and packages. "Yes. Now, go away—aren't you off duty?"

He rose lithely to his feet, snatching up a few boxes as he did so. "I had a late surgery on an accident victim. And, since you've been avoiding me, I—"

"I have not," she interrupted quickly, careful to keep her face averted lest he see her guilty expression. "I've been busy. *Really* busy."

He was quiet for a few beats before saying mildly, "So you said. But, contrary to what you think, I didn't come here for the express purpose of ravishing you. Delightful though it's been."

She sent him a quick glare before turning away to hide her hot cheeks. "Then why *did* you come?"

"I need a date."

She stumbled and grabbed hold of the shelf at her elbow. "A *date*?" Why she was surprised and disappointed, Dani didn't know. She was back on the wagon, after all. "Dr. Sexy needs a *date*?"

His mouth twisted wryly. "My mother has forced me to buy a couple of tickets to a charity dinner tomorrow night and I need a partner."

"So…*any* woman will do?" she asked, casually pretending to count bags of Ringer's lactate when her brain was still stuck on the fact that all he wanted was a date.

When he didn't reply she peeked at him over her shoulder. He was leaning casually against the opposite shelves, watching her with an exasperated expression.

"Actually, no," he drawled dryly. "I want to take *you*—although I'm not sure why, especially as you've been ignoring me."

She blinked at him and tried to deny that his

words had sent pleasure rushing through her. She couldn't. "But what about my embargo?"

His sigh suggested she was an idiot, because anyone could see she'd fallen off the wagon a second time. With *him*. In record time, too.

His voice dropped a couple of octaves. "Come with me."

A small frown creased the area between her brows even as a shiver eased down her spine. She ignored the unpleasant lurching of her stomach. "I…uh… I don't know, Dylan. Those dinners aren't really my thing." Mostly because it was a world she'd run from and had no desire to re-enter.

His eyes darkened. "Please?"

And suddenly, queasy stomach aside, Dani realized she couldn't resist a pleading Dylan. "All right," she muttered, folding like a cheap suitcase. "I suppose it's a formal dinner?"

"Very." A smile bloomed across his handsome face as he leaned forward to drop a quick kiss on her startled mouth. "I'll pick you up at seven."

CHAPTER NINE

THE ORCHESTRA HIRED for the charity event segued into a waltz as Dylan pushed his way through Vancouver's social elite. He'd left Dani with Cole's sister Maddie and her date, to find some champagne, and he was in a hurry to get back.

His afternoon surgery had run late and to save time he'd had his mother book a suite at the Regency, where the event was taking place. He'd sent word to Dani to make use of the facility and by the time he'd emerged from the adjoining room, white tie stuffed in his pocket and struggling with his cufflinks, she'd been ready and waiting.

Dylan couldn't ever remember feeling as if he'd been hit on the head with a brick at the sight of a woman in an evening gown before. But, dressed in a long sheath of silvery stretch lace and beaded flower work, she'd literally taken his breath away.

In the sleeveless dress, its scalloped neckline molding perfectly to her full breasts and slender curvy body, she'd looked both elegant and so enormously desirable that his only thought had been to strip her out of it and miss the dinner entirely.

Her dark hair was swept up into some kind of complicated style that left tiny spiral curls framing her face, softening the delicate lines of her jaw. She'd applied make-up with a light hand but the effect was stunning, rendering him speechless as he'd stared into deep gray eyes that were wide and smokily seductive.

He'd felt as though the earth had given way beneath his feet and he'd been left free-falling through an alien universe. It had been all he could do not to stammer like a fool.

"You look…*stunning*," he'd murmured when she'd taken over the task of fitting his cufflinks.

The flush creeping up her chest and neck had tempted him to trace its origins, past the scalloped neckline to the full swells of her breasts.

Leaning closer, he'd buried his nose in her throat. "And you smell even better."

"Not as good as you," she'd muttered, her quick

smile turning her eyes silver as she'd slipped his white tie from his pocket to fit it around his neck.

"No," he'd grumbled, yanking at the white waistcoat of the black penguin suit his mother had had delivered to the suite. "I look like a damn waiter."

"A very classy one," she'd agreed with a giggle, ducking away when he'd reached for her.

Thinking his unscheduled surgery a convenient excuse for the fact that they were going to be *very* late, he'd caught her at the door and kissed her until she was flushed and dazed. After the way she'd ignored him these past couple of weeks, it had been very gratifying to have her melting into him.

"What's that wicked smile for, darling?"

A husky feminine voice interrupted his musings and Dylan turned to see his mother, bearing down on him with a determined gleam in her green eyes.

"It's the same one you used to wear when you were plotting mischief as a boy."

"I'm just thinking of all the lovely zeroes you're going to add to your foundation's coffers," he drawled, thinking there were some things a mother didn't need to know.

"I know," she said happily, reaching up to kiss his cheek. "Isn't it wonderful? I have a long list of recipients we can help with the proceeds."

He dropped an affectionate kiss on her brow before looking around for his father. "Where's Dad?"

"Oh, talking to some crony or another. I gave him strict instructions to badger them all for large donations this year."

"I'm sure you did." He chuckled, imagining his father—owner and CEO of the largest shipping company in the Pacific North-West—meekly listening while his wife of thirty six years rapped out orders. "And I'm just as sure he's doing exactly what you told him to."

"Of course he is," Vivian St. James said archly. "If he knows what's good for him—which is more than I can say for my children."

He sent his mother a dry look, knowing what she was doing but pretending otherwise. "What have the girls done now?"

"I'm talking about my *son*," she retorted, slipping her hand through his arm and smiling a greeting to nearby acquaintances. Her gaze was direct and slightly narrowed when she looked up at him. "Please tell me you didn't come alone like last time."

His mouth twisted wryly as he admitted, "I didn't come alone."

Her face instantly broke into a pleased smile. "Ooh! And I suppose *she's* responsible for that wicked smile I caught on your handsome face?"

"Mom…" he began, horrified to discover his face heating beneath her dancing gaze.

"She *is*!" She laughed at his discomfort and nudged him with her shoulder, her eyes sparkling with delight. "And…? When are you going to introduce me?"

"I'll do it now, if you promise not to embarrass her or start planning the wedding."

"Oh, silly boy!" She chortled scornfully. "When will you learn? I've already planned your wedding. I'm just waiting for you to meet the right woman."

"Behave," he warned her, finally catching sight of Dani and Maddie talking to— *"Damn."* He scowled, recognizing the man as the son of one of the partners at the law firm his father used.

He knew Richard Ashton-Hall from school but they'd never run in the same crowd. The spiteful, opinionated boy had grown into a condescending egotistical man, who used his social status as a member of one of the leading legal families in Vancouver to lord it over what he called "the peasants." He liked getting what he wanted and bullied people until he did.

Dylan had heard enough unsavory rumors about the man to know that he wouldn't want him dating his sisters. There was something unpleasant in the way he looked at a woman—as though he was stripping her naked with one arrogant glance and finding her either wanting or the perfect candidate as his new plaything.

And he *really* didn't like the way he was looking at Dani now. It roused primitive emotions he'd have sworn he didn't possess.

Chief among them was the urge to smash his fist into that smirking salon-tanned face. His fingers curled into tight fists, because he absolutely did not like the shocked, furious expression on Maddie's face or the rigid line of Dani's spine.

"What is it, darling?" Vivian James asked in concern, no doubt feeling the abrupt tension in the arm she was holding. She looked around in alarm and said, "Oh, look, there's Madeleine… My goodness." Her eyes widened. "She looks quite fierce, doesn't she? Frankly, I'm not surprised. Not with that dreadful man looking at her companion like that—" She stopped abruptly, her gaze snapping from the unfolding drama to her son's face. "It's her, isn't it?"

He nodded. "Yes, that's Dani."

"Well then," his mother urged. "What are you waiting for?" She gave his arm a firm yank. "Go and rescue her from that awful boy."

In seconds he was striding up behind Dani, not realizing that he'd practically shoved people out of the way in his haste to get to her. He was still a short distance away when he heard Maddie snarl, "Why don't you crawl back under the rock you emerged from, you slimy toad?"

Ashton-Hall, looking like a blond male model, dismissed Maddie with a flick of one perfectly manicured hand, his ice-blue eyes never leaving Dani's face.

"Get lost, Madeleine. I'm trying to have a conversation with my...*wife.*"

His eyes were sliding over Dani's body with a knowing predatory light and it had a snarl rising in Dylan's throat. His words—and Dani's visible flinch—shocked him into halting a few feet from the group. He could only blink back the red tide of rage rising up inside his head.

What?

"Ex!" Maddie yelped, bristling with fury and looking as if she wanted to strike him. "*Ex*-wife, you mean."

Dylan didn't realize he'd taken another step until his mother's hand closed around his fist. "No fighting, darling," she murmured in his ear. "Even if I'd be cheering you on from the sidelines."

The words and the supportive squeeze settled him, and he stepped up behind Dani with amazing casualness to slide his palm up her back. She jolted at his touch, a quiver racing through her tense body.

Deliberately ignoring the other man, he dipped his head when she looked up. He caught a brief impression of her eyes as he touched his mouth to hers. Her lips quivered and he sank into the kiss as though they didn't have an audience.

"Sorry I took so long," he said, when he finally lifted his head. "The bar's busy."

He was pleased to see his very public display of affection had wild color replacing her pale distress. He took his time to look around at the group watching them with varying expressions—Ashton-Hall showed shock mixed with fury at having his prey snatched away, the lawyer's date was looking wide-eyed at the simmering undercurrents, and Maddie... Well, she'd never looked more gleefully triumphant.

"You know Dr. St. James, don't you?" Maddie said, so sweetly that Dylan felt his blood sugar rise. "He's the leading reconstruction orthopedic surgeon at St. Mary's. Oh, yes—and I'm sure you know his *father*: Ruben James, CEO and owner of—"

"Ashton-Hall," Dylan interrupted with a curt nod, his hand sliding down Dani's trembling arm to link with her fingers. He lifted their clasped hands to brush his lips across her icy-cold knuckles, his hard eyes taking in the way the other man's narrowed gaze took in the intimate gesture.

Her fingers jerked convulsively in his.

"Well, well..." Ashton-Hall drawled softly, his golden good looks hardening into something unpleasant. "My dear, lovely wife...*ex*-wife," he corrected, with a patently false smile of apology in Maddie's direction, "has managed to land herself a bigger, fatter, juicier fish after all." He turned to Dylan. "My...uh...congratulations."

His voice suggested otherwise as he flicked

her a contemptuous glance and Dylan bit back a snarl, because beneath the contempt was an unhealthy possessiveness that made his skin crawl.

"I wonder what he would say if he knew about what a disappointment you were in…" He paused for dramatic effect, his ice-blue eyes gleaming with malice at the sound of Dani's abruptly indrawn breath, audible in the tense silence.

"I suggest you stop right there," Dylan warned softly.

"In our marriage." He blinked at Dylan, as though surprised. "What did you *think* I was going to say?"

"Nothing I'd want to hear from a man who likes to hit women," he said smoothly, and felt a savage satisfaction when the man's unnatural tan reddened, then paled.

"How did you—? She *told* you that?"

"No," Dylan drawled smoothly, despite the fury sweeping through him. "*You* just did."

Ashton-Hall's hands curled into fists and his mouth twisted into something ugly as his gaze zeroed in on Dani. Dylan felt her stiffen beside him, as though she was bracing herself.

Then Richard suddenly laughed, all suave urbanity that invited everyone to see the irony of the situation. His eyebrows rose arrogantly. "Maybe," he said to Dylan, "when you're done slumming with the Ice Princess we can compare notes."

Dylan heard his mother's outraged inhalation through a red mist, and before he could think he'd drawn back his arm and punched Ashton-Hall in his smug, sneering face.

The crunch of the man's nose beneath his fist was the most satisfying moment of Dylan's life, dulling the pain radiating up his arm.

The shocked gasps of the people around them snapped Dani out of her misery. Ignoring the man lying on the hotel foyer floor, she grabbed Dylan's arm and held on as he took another step forward. Fury blasted from him like a nuclear explosion, the force of it vibrating through the steely muscles beneath her hand.

"Dylan." Her horrified gaze took in the attention they were attracting. *"Stop!* It doesn't matter."

He was breathing hard, his green eyes a blaze of fury in his stony face. "Doesn't *matter*?" he snarled, taking another step toward Richard. *"He* was the one—" He inhaled sharply and practically ground his next words into pieces as he stared at the other man, menace pumping off him in great billowing clouds. "I'm going to kill him."

Her face flamed with mortification, and quick tears blurred her vision because she would give anything—*anything*—for him not to know. "Dylan, *please*," she urged, her voice low and urgent. "Let it go. It doesn't matter."

"He put his hands on you in *anger*," he snarled, his jaw practically popping with fury. "Of *course* it matters."

"*No.* It doesn't," she argued gently. "Not anymore. Because *he* doesn't matter."

She closed her hands over his clenched fist, hoping to dispel the violence pounding through him and caught the wince he couldn't quite prevent. Frowning, she looked down at his hand and sucked in a shocked breath when she saw the damaged, swelling knuckles.

"Look what you've done to your hand. How can you—?"

He caught her shaking fingers and waited until her distraught gaze met his. "It was worth it."

"I hope you still think so when I sue the pants off you," the man on the floor snarled, draw-

ing everyone's attention. They'd all but forgotten him. Flushing with embarrassed fury at the
curious stares they were receiving, he lurched
to his feet and spat out. "I'll sue you until even
your grandchildren are paying through the nose.
I'll ruin you. I'll—"

"Oh, be quiet, Richard," snapped Dani, suddenly furious with both of them for causing a
scene with their masculine posturing. "You're
an ass."

She shoved at Dylan while her ex-husband
mopped the blood from his nose with a pristine
handkerchief.

"And as for *you*—" She probed his hand gently.
"You need ice and maybe a lobotomy."

Black spots hovered at the edge of her vision
and she sucked in a shaky breath to dispel the
odd dizziness and shaky stomach.

"He'll do it," she said in urgent undertones. "I
know he will. It's happened before."

"Let him try," Dylan said, unconcerned, wrapping his free hand around her neck and nudging
her chin up with his thumb. His expression was
concerned as he studied her face. "You're pale."

She wrapped her fingers around his wrist, the
feel of his warm skin and steady pulse beneath

her fingers stabilizing her. "I'm fine. Which is more than I can say for your hand. Let me get you some ice."

"This is all very sweet and sickening," Richard snarled furiously. "But what about *me*? He broke my nose."

"You should thank him," Maddie snorted unsympathetically. "It'll give your face character. Something the rest of you lacks."

Richard ignored her. "Expect to hear from me next week," he said.

He stepped close in a move Dani recognized from her marriage. It was one that had never failed to make her knees quake.

He smirked at her instinctive retreat before she ordered her feet to stop. "It's going to be fun watching you squirm."

Dani ignored the threat. "Try it and I'll expose you *and* your sleazy club," she said softly.

Richard froze, his eyes narrowing. "What club?" he lied smoothly, grimacing with distaste as blood continued to flow from his nose.

"Your little swingers'—"

"You wouldn't," he interrupted, with an unconcerned scoff that couldn't quite mask the panic in his eyes as he sent a quick glance around to see if anyone had heard.

It was in that moment she realized that he was nothing but a spoilt bully who used his family's legal reputation as a tool to intimidate and scare. Standing up to him suddenly seemed like the most natural thing in the world. Because he couldn't hurt her. Not anymore.

"You're forgetting the non-disclosure agreement," he reminded her coolly as he straightened his tie and brushed off his jacket.

"If you recall," she reminded him quietly, refusing to be cowed, "I declined to sign it."

Conscious of her trembling knees, she turned away. But his hand shot out, his grip cruel as he yanked her against him.

"And *you*," he warned silkily, "might recall what happened then."

Dylan's fingers immediately clamped down on Richard's wrist and with a girlish squeak he loosened his grip immediately.

Dani stilled, a frown pulling at her brows as she resisted Dylan's efforts to pull her away. "What are you talking about?"

His gaze turned malicious. "That drunk driver who drove you off the road?" His lips curled into a hard, cruel smile as he mouthed, *That was me*, before sauntering off.

Oblivious to warm hands settling on her arms, Dani felt the words rushing over her like a swarm of bees. They pierced her skin, leaving their poison to tear through her fragile armor, leaving her with a sick certainty that dispelled any doubts she might have had about that night.

The blood drained abruptly from her head and her knees sagged. She heard Maddie's startled yelp even as Dylan caught her against himself.

"Dani!" he rasped, his deep voice laced with a concern that battered at her, tightening her chest until she couldn't breathe.

Her heart swelled, desperate to pump blood to her numbed limbs. Her ears buzzed and her fingers tingled as the ballroom receded. Unaware of the wounded moan rising up her throat, Dani pressed a shaking hand to her breastbone, hoping to keep her pounding heart from exploding through her ribs. Keep it from leaving a gaping hole in her chest.

She sucked in a tortured breath. She had to get away. She had to—

Nausea burned her throat like acid, and with a desperate cry she shoved herself free, lurching away from him as she frantically searched for the nearest exit. She felt Dylan's hand on her arm, heard him say…*something*. But she slapped a hand over her mouth, snatched up her long skirt and ran toward the ladies' restroom.

She heard Dylan's stunned curse as the door swung shut behind her, barely making it into an open stall before her stomach emptied violently. Collapsing to the floor, Dani hung over the toilet as her stomach continued to heave, as though to dispel the awful truth swamping her.

Richard… *Richard* was responsible for the accident that had taken her baby and left her uterus scarred. A sob caught in her throat.

Through the roaring in her ears she vaguely heard voices behind her—a woman's voice urgently calling, "*Dani!* Dani, where are you?" But she couldn't, *couldn't* respond. She was too busy retching, devastated by the knowledge that the man who'd once promised to love and protect her had—

She was barely aware that she was sobbing, her chest heaving as she wished…no, *prayed*… the floor would open and swallow her whole.

Then frantic hands were reaching for her. Hands that shook as Maddie murmured brokenly, "I had a feeling this would happen one day. This city isn't big enough that you can avoid him forever."

"Richard..." Dani rasped, grabbing Maddie's arm in a shaky grip.

"Yeah, he's a colossal ass—what's new?" her friend snapped, gently wiping Dani's mouth even as someone else pressed a cold cloth to her burning forehead.

Eyes huge and dark with shock, Dani whispered, "It was *him.*"

"Yeah, I wish he'd drop dead too... Wait!" Maddie frowned, her eyes confused as she crouched at Dani's side. *"What* was him?"

"He... He..." Dani swallowed past the burning ball of glass shards in her throat. "That night... *He* was the drunk driver."

For a moment Maddie stared at her uncomprehendingly, then she sucked in a shocked breath. "Are you saying...?" Her eyes widened. *"That's crazy!* He wouldn't— He— Dani, that's *insane.*"

A sob rose in Dani's throat as she gave a jerky nod. "He told me...just now," she said, feeling the shock of it swamp her. "It was *him* that night—*he* caused the accident." She shivered, recalling it. "He was so f-furious with me for embarrassing him in front of his friends. But I didn't think he could—could he?" She sucked in a shaky breath and felt the walls closing in on her. "C-could he really be capable of th—that?"

A snarl of fury burst from her friend's lips as she lurched to her feet. "I'm going to kill him," she vowed, looking murderous. "I'm going to make him wish he'd never been born. I'm going to—"

"Maddie, darling." A low, soothing voice interrupted from somewhere close. "Can you put a hold on those bloodthirsty plans long enough to get Dani out of here?"

Maddie blinked rapidly before sucking in a steadying breath. They were attracting unwanted attention. "Oh, right…" she said, bending to wrap an arm around Dani and pull her to her feet.

But Dani's legs weren't working properly and she swayed dizzily, the blood draining from her head as prickly heat washed over her. She gave a low moan and thrust out a hand to grab the doorframe but the floor dipped and rolled and the walls melted away.

Then firm, warm fingers closed around hers and she blinked up into concerned green eyes that even in her shocked state reminded her of

Dylan's. Green eyes set in the beautiful face of an older woman.

"Come on, darling," she said, gently but firmly pulling Dani from the cubicle. "We left Dylan outside, and if I know my son he'll come barging in here if we don't walk out in under a minute."

Dani's eyes widened and she gasped. "You're Dylan's—?"

"Mother," the older woman finished.

"Oh God," she whimpered. She sucked in a fortifying breath and managed to get out, "You… you *saw* all that?"

Her words sounded tinny to her own ears, and even as she saw compassion filling those green eyes a great wave of prickling heat swamped her.

With a mortified moan, she slid to the floor.

CHAPTER TEN

DANI SURFACED TO find herself lying on something soft. Somewhere close, people spoke in hushed tones. She strained her ears but couldn't make out anything other than suppressed fury and concern.

For a couple of beats she wondered why there were people in her bedroom and tried to turn over, to block out the noise but a soft hand held her still as a cold cloth was pressed against her forehead.

Brow wrinkling in confusion, she reached up to swipe at the annoyance but warm fingers trapped hers.

"It's all right, Dani," a gentle, feminine voice soothed. "Take it easy. I *can* call you Dani, can't I?" The low voice quivered with amusement. "Anyone who can turn my son into an avenging pugilist one minute and a panicked wreck the next is someone I'd very much like to meet."

Something brushed her cheek.

"Come on, sweetheart, open your eyes before he calls an ambulance."

Memory returned with the speed of a freight train and she lurched upward, her eyes flying open to see—*Oh God*—Dylan's mother, her green eyes filled with maternal concern and curiosity. A few feet away Dylan paced, his body vibrating with fury as Maddie spoke in urgent undertones.

Panic rose up to blot out everything, because she knew—just *knew*—what Maddie was telling Dylan. All the sordid details of her marriage.

Her stomach roiled in greasy protest. *"Nooo!"* she moaned, trying to scramble off the sofa, as though she could physically stop the words from emerging.

Seeing the direction of her panicked gaze, Dylan's mother caught her, calling out, *"Children!"* in a firm voice that children everywhere recognized and instantly obeyed. "You're upsetting Dani."

As one, they spun around. Within two strides Dylan was at her side, one large hand engulfing hers as he dropped down beside her. Intense green eyes swept over her, cataloging her condition.

"You're looking a little better," he rasped, his fingers lacing convulsively through hers. His dark gaze caught and held hers as though he could see through to her soul. "How do you feel?"

"F-fine," she stammered, trying to disengage her hand from his and put a little distance between them. She needed to leave before she made a bigger spectacle of herself than she already had. And in front of his *mother*!

His fingers tightened. "You're lying."

She froze and blinked her surprise, her gaze flying to his mother, who was watching them with wide, curious eyes and a strange little smile on her face.

"What a terrible thing to say," she accused in a low voice, pulling unsuccessfully at her hand. "And let go—you're embarrassing me."

"And *you're* making me look bad in front of my mother and Maddie." He lifted his free hand to cup her chin but Dani grabbed it, wincing at the sight of his bruised, swollen knuckles.

"Why haven't you iced this?"

"I had other things on my mind," he growled. "Like you fainting in the women's restroom."

He shoved impatient fingers through his hair.

Dani was shocked at the pallor beneath his skin and the perceptible tremor in his fingers.

"You have no idea how I felt when I saw you passed out on the floor."

She rolled her eyes and distracted herself by taking his hand and gently probing his injury. An injury sustained on *her* behalf.

"It's probably just a little virus, that's all," she assured him, looking up to see Maddie and Dylan's mother watching them with wide, fascinated eyes. Because she was angry with Maddie, for spilling her secrets, she said coolly, "Dylan needs an ice pack."

Maddie's gaze narrowed at the silent rebuke but didn't look too disturbed when she gave a nod and left the room.

"Don't blame Maddie. She was just trying to help—" Dylan began.

He was cut off when Dani hissed, "*Help?* How can airing my disaster of a marriage be helping?"

Clearly taken aback by her vehemence, Dylan hardened his jaw. "You should have told me yourself."

"Why? Because we slept together?" She abruptly cut off the rest of her words because they still had an audience. *Oh God*—his mother was listening with rapt attention to their exchange.

Face flaming, Dani rose unsteadily to her feet but when she took a step away from him Dylan grabbed her hand and yanked her back to the sofa.

"Dylan!"

"Sit," he ordered, pressing his fingers to her pulse. "I'm worried about you. When last did you eat?"

Her tongue snaked out to dampen her dry lips and instantly the older woman was there, offering a glass of water. "I'm fine," she repeated, taking the glass. "But thank you," she said quietly. "For your concern."

"Yes, Mom, thanks—but you really should get back to the ball. Aren't you in charge of proceedings?"

"Oh, don't worry about me, darling," the older woman said, brushing aside his concern. "Janice Hetherington will take over."

"No, please," Dani said, her fingers tightening around the glass. "Mrs. St. James, I insist. I'm just sorry you had to witness—" She licked her lips nervously and slid her gaze sideways to include the man at her side. "Well…*that*. I'm sorry I ruined your function."

"Call me Vivian, dear. And you haven't ruined anything. Besides, *you* have nothing to apologize for," Dylan's mother declared firmly. "It was all Richard." Her eyes went to her son. "And maybe Dylan too. *But*," she added, when Dani opened her mouth to leap to his defense, "if *he* hadn't punched him, *I* would have."

To say Dani was shocked by the swift rejoinder was an understatement but the glint in the older woman's eye told her she would have done it if her son hadn't beat her to it.

Vivian St. James' eyes bounced between Dylan and Dani for a couple of beats before she sighed. "Fine, I know when to make a graceful exit. *But*," she said, pointing a slender finger at Dylan, "I expect you to bring Dani to meet your father."

And with that she dropped a gentle kiss on Dani's upturned cheek, arched a peremptory brow at her son and left the room in a swish of skirts.

For several moments Dani stared at the closed door, before turning to see Dylan watching her with an odd combination of concern, satisfaction and amusement.

She narrowed her eyes. "What?"

"My mother likes you."

She puffed out her red cheeks. "I have no idea why—I embarrassed her."

He chuckled. "No, *I* did. But since I brought you along she'll forgive me." His hand was warm and gentle as he cupped her chin and tilted it up. "You're still looking a little pale. What's up, Dani? Talk to me."

Unable to handle the gentle concern and the look in his eyes, Dani pulled away and rose. She needed to put a little distance between them before she forgot they were only having a wild affair.

She inhaled carefully. "Like I said, it's probably just a virus or something." She smoothed unsteady hands down her dress and aimed a shaky smile in his direction. "I like your mother." She bit her lip and pressed a hand against her stomach. "But maybe it would be better if I left."

With a muffled curse Dylan surged to his feet and took a step toward her, coming to an abrupt halt when she sucked in a startled breath and stumbled backward into a nearby chair. She threw out a hand to catch herself before she took another tumble and added to the evening's humiliation.

* * *

"Why do you *do* that?" he demanded. "Why do you pull away just when I think we're getting somewhere?" He knew he sounded frustrated and bewildered.

She licked her lips nervously and edged toward the door. "Dylan—"

Dylan shoved his hands in his pockets, the abrupt movement filled with frustration. "I'd never lift my hand to a woman, so you can just stop right there. I'm not like your ex."

Dani's spine snapped straight. "I didn't say you were," she shot back.

Dylan was pleased to see angry color flood her pale cheeks, a sparkle replacing the remoteness in her eyes.

"Don't put words in my mouth."

Anger, he decided, was preferable to that wounded wariness that made him want to find her ex and break his nose all over again. And maybe a few other bones as well.

"It's hard not to when you seldom put any there yourself."

She sucked in a harsh breath. "What's that supposed to mean?"

"Nothing." He sighed, turning away. It wasn't

her fault that he wanted more than she was prepared to give, and beating at her with his exasperation would only cause her to withdraw even more. "I'm just wondering why you never told me what he did."

"You expect me to spill my guts just because we *s-slept* together?"

Annoyed, Dylan shoved a hand through his hair, wincing when his swollen knuckles protested. "No..." He sighed again. "But I might have handled the situation better, handled *you* better, if I'd known."

"What makes you think I need you—or anyone—to 'handle' me?" she demanded. "I can handle myself, Dylan. I'm an adult. I don't *need* you to fight my battles for me. I don't need *anyone* to fight my battles for me."

Her unspoken words, *I don't need anyone*, hung in the air between them and he wondered if she really believed it. If she did, he'd have a hard time convincing her to trust him.

Frustrated, he flung words over his shoulder. "I couldn't just stand by and let him slash at you like that, Dani." He faced her and demanded, "What kind of man would do that?"

Her body slowly lost its rigidity and she had

the grace to grimace in apology. "I'm embar-rassed," she muttered, wrapping her arms around her torso as her gaze slid away. "I humiliated myself." Her chin lifted. "I embarrassed your mother and now you…you—" She pressed her lips together.

"And now I what?"

She spun away, the rigid lines of her body ra-diating new tension. "Richard isn't the kind of man who handles humiliation well," she snapped over her shoulder. "He'll—"

"I know exactly what kind of man he is," he interrupted smoothly, annoyed that she would think the lawyer had intimidated him.

"He'll do what he says," she added, as though he hadn't spoken. "He'll pad the truth and come up with a dozen witnesses to corroborate his lies."

"I don't care about him, Dani. I care about *you*. And I care about what he said that had you faint-ing in the bathroom, that upset you so much that you're repairing those walls around you faster than I can tear them down."

His hands settled on her shoulders. He felt the bones delicate and fragile beneath his hands. He wanted to wrap his arms around her and wished she would lean on him, take what he offered.

"What hold does he have on you?"

Dylan's hands were warm, firm and gentle as they cupped her shoulders. His touch, the deep tone of his voice, made her eyes sting with longing. It would be so easy to lean on him, to take what he offered.

But she couldn't. Didn't dare. Because…because she wanted it too much. And wanting things too much was a sure-fire way to get her heart broken. But he was there, so steady and strong that she couldn't resist turning into him.

"He doesn't," she murmured, sliding her hands up to his shoulders to tunnel unsteady fingers through his hair. "Not anymore."

With her eyes on his she lifted onto her toes, her body sliding against his as she pressed a soft, tentative kiss to the corner of his mouth. For just an instant he resisted. She could see in his eyes that he wanted to argue but then he gave a low, agonized groan and wrapped his arms around her in one jerky movement. His mouth, hard and seeking, closed over hers in a searing kiss that belied the abrupt strength in his arms, the tension in his body.

This, she thought with a shiver of excitement, was all she could give him.

"Come home with me," he said, and groaned, his hands urging her closer, as though she was infinitely precious and fragile, smoothing a path up the length of her back, his body vibrating with heat and urgency.

She could feel his heart pounding beneath her palm and wondered if he felt what she did—a sense of rightness that scared her even as it made her yearn for what could never be.

With a rough growl he dragged his lips along the line of her jaw. "No…upstairs. I…can't wait."

Dani, lost in the pleasure of his mouth, fought with the buttons of his waistcoat and then his shirt. "Here," she demanded, shoving her hands between the plackets to slide them over his hot skin. *"Now."*

With a savage curse he swept her off her feet, and together they dropped onto the sofa against the wall. He shoved a thigh between hers.

"God, I've missed you," he rasped against her lips, before taking her mouth in a kiss that was abruptly impatient. "I want this…*you.*"

And, thrilled by this new dark edginess, Dani lifted her mouth to his and gave him everything.

Sagging against the bathroom wall, Dani swiped the back of her shaky hand across her mouth. It was the second time she'd lost the contents of her stomach in the past twenty-four hours, and she couldn't remember how often she'd lost them over the past few weeks.

Maybe it was time to admit it probably *wasn't* a virus, or even stress. Maybe it *could* still be stress, she admitted with a grimace. They hadn't yet heard from Richard, and that usually wasn't a good thing. But, although the waiting was exhausting, it wasn't nearly as terrifying as waiting for Dylan to lose interest and dump her for someone more suitable. Someone more beautiful, more exciting, more...*everything*.

Someone not likely to embarrass him in public.

Although, she admitted reluctantly, he seemed to be showing no signs of losing interest. Instead, every day he seemed to be...*more*. More patient, more passionate, more... *God*...more tender, she thought with a delicious shiver. He touched her more often—and not just during sex—as though he wanted her to know he was there. Wanted her to get used to the weight of his hand, the heat of his body, even in a crowd of people.

And he'd made her crave him, she admitted with a touch of panic. Crave the way she'd awake locked in his arms. Crave *being* with him. And if that didn't scare her enough, the way he kept hijacking her thoughts did. She thought about him at the most inconvenient times and she hated it. Hated it that he'd come to mean so much…

Oh God, she was in trouble. The kind that could break a girl's heart if she wasn't careful.

But Dani had learned the hard way to be very careful. Careful not to let the expression in his eyes and the touch of his hand as it smoothed the length of her spine affect anything more than her senses. And she was being extra careful with her heart, which was locked up tight and safe.

And that was a good thing. A very good thing. Or she'd be—

"So…" An annoyed voice interrupted her panicked thoughts. "When are you going to stop hiding in the supply room or the bathroom and tell me what's going on?"

Dani opened her eyes to see two sneakers beneath the stall door—one propped over the other as though their owner leaned casually against the wall. She groaned. Amy gave new meaning to the word *persistent*.

She rolled her head against the wall, too exhausted to shove at the damp hair that had fallen into her face. "I'm fine," she rasped through her burning throat.

The nurse muttered a succinct curse. "You're still sick, aren't you?"

Yeah, a little voice answered, *love-sick.*

No, no, no! she denied, aghast. *Nothing of the sort*. She was just a little stressed. Waiting for Richard to strike *always* made her tense.

"Of course I'm not sick," Dani scoffed weakly because it was patently obvious to everyone that she hadn't been herself lately. "I'm just hoping to escape your endless questions. I'm fit as a fiddle."

Her friend made a rude sound in the back of her throat. "Then you won't mind getting checked out by Rachel."

Rachel, an ER physician in her fifties, was the shift supervisor.

"Don't be ridiculous, Amy."

Dani impatiently brushed her suggestion aside and pushed to her feet. Cursing the exhaustion that made her want to lie down and sleep for a week, she opened the door.

"I don't need to see Rachel or anyone else. I'm just feeling a little under the weather, that's all."

"Okay," the nurse said.

She sounded so agreeable that Dani relaxed as she headed for the row of basins to wash her hands and rinse her mouth. Too soon it seemed, because then came Amy's next words.

"If you won't see Rachel, then I want you to use this. Right now."

Dani sent a frowning look over her shoulder, her eyes widening as she saw the slender box her friend held out.

"Seriously?" she demanded with a snort. "You want me to pee on a stick?"

Blue eyes stared back, level and serious. "Yes."

Dani rolled her eyes and pulled off a strip of paper toweling to dab her face. "You know that's not possible."

"Because you have Asherman's?" Amy asked mildly. "Or because you haven't been getting any with a certain gorgeous orthopedic surgeon?"

Dani quickly looked around the bathroom, relieved to see it was empty. "Well, because… Because…" she stuttered, then snapped her mouth closed when she couldn't think of a single reply other than *You know why.*

She turned away, pretending she was on top of things when the truth was she felt as though she was going down for the third time.

"Unprotected sex?" Amy yelped.

Dani gave a guilty start. A quick look over her shoulder showed her friend staring at her with open-mouthed shock.

"Seriously?" She shook her head as though to dispel the image. "Are you *insane*?"

Face flaming, Dani squawked, "A condom broke and then…and then we didn't…um…" She rolled her eyes and snickered, because she couldn't help feeling like a teenager facing her mother after being caught having sex in the sitting room. "We…um…didn't bother after that. *Mom.*"

Amy snorted. "Let's forget the safety issues for just a moment, shall we?" Grabbing Dani's wrist, she pulled her back toward the stall she'd just vacated.

Resisting, Dani huffed out an exasperated laugh. "Amy—"

The nurse stopped and spun around so suddenly that Dani plowed into her.

"I care about you."

The hitch in her friend's voice, the concern, silenced any retort she might have made.

"You've lost weight, you're pale and you have dark circles under your eyes. You're a mess and I'm worried about you."

After a couple dozen heartbeats Dani sighed and surrendered. She didn't want to tell her friend that she was afraid she was in love with a man who was way out of her league—a man who was a member of a social class she could never belong to. Didn't *want* to belong to, she reminded herself.

"All right," she growled, grabbing the pregnancy test and stomping into the stall. She turned and jabbed it into the air. "If only to prove that your theory is totally off the wall. I'm a little run-down and I can't shake this virus. That's all."

Secure in the knowledge that she was right, she shut the door smartly in her friend's face. *She* was the doctor, wasn't she? Surely she'd be able to tell the difference between a virus and early pregnancy? Even if it was possible.

Which it wasn't.

Ten minutes later, however, she was staring in shock at the twin pink stripes in the results window. Her knees wobbled, her ears buzzed and her head felt as if it was two feet above the rest of her body.

"But… But that's—"

"Impossible?" Amy demanded, her face alternating between delight and shock that probably mirrored Dani's.

"But…but… Dr. Cartwright said… He said—"

"Well, clearly he was wrong," Amy interrupted, practically shoving the stick under Dani's nose. "Doctors sometimes are, you know. They aren't infallible and they aren't God."

Dani refused to believe it. "These things aren't definitive either, Amy," she said briskly, grabbing the box to check the use-by date. "They're often defective and give false positives. I have Asherman's."

"Well, clearly you don't," Amy retorted smartly. "And to make certain, why don't you schedule an appointment with Dr. Dawson? Getting a second opinion won't hurt." Her eyebrows arched challengingly. "*Will* it?"

Yes, dammit, it *would* hurt. Especially if she got her hopes up and it turned out to be a faulty test. It would… She'd be devastated.

"Fine," she said calmly. "But I'm telling you it's a false positive. I'm not pregnant."

She shook her head firmly and for an instant wondered who she was trying to convince. Herself or Amy.

"I *can't* be pregnant. It's just not possible."

She was pregnant.

Fierce joy warred with disbelief and panic as Dani gripped the steering wheel until her fingers ached. Driving off the ferry at Departure Bay, Nanaimo, she was scarcely aware of the stream of cars and throng of people around her.

For God's sake, she lectured herself silently as her heart pounded and her vision wavered. *Get a grip.* She was pregnant, not dying. But *damn* if she wasn't hyperventilating—in a good way—at the notion of life growing in her belly. And hyperventilating—*not* in a good way—at the thought of telling Dylan.

A keening moan escaped before she could shove it back. It was the very last conversation she wanted to have. Not after assuring him they were safe. Not after the best month of her life. And like an idiot, she even found herself dreaming of a future with Dylan—which was ridiculous, especially as she'd been the one to insist they were temporary. He'd think she was trying to trap him and he'd be furious. She couldn't blame him but it would be the end of anything good between them.

Her belly clenched, then rolled greasily with panic. Could it really be true? Perhaps what she and Nicole Dawson had seen was a cyst…or a tumor? She couldn't be so lucky as to be pregnant, could she? Not after the past few years of hell. Not after that devastating diagnosis.

Maybe she should have another scan to be sure. Maybe the sonar had been faulty and maybe—

A bubble of hysterical laughter popped, loud enough to startle her. *She was losing it.* Maybe she should just book herself into the psych ward because she was clearly having a mental breakdown.

There was no mistake.

She'd seen that little blob on the sonar herself, heard the unmistakable sound of a fetal heartbeat through the roar of blood in her ears. And, despite the shock, she'd distinctly heard the gynecologist say, "Congratulations, Dani, you're pregnant."

Nicole had laughed and pointed to the monitor, where the tiny buds attached to the blob were moving like crazy, as if Dani's child was waving at her and saying, *Hey, Mom, look at me. I'm here.*

"Look at that," Nicole had said, moving closer to the monitor. "I've never seen anything like it in such a young fetus." She'd grinned as she'd tapped a few commands into her computer. "This little one's already a fighter."

And in that instant Dani had fallen completely in love.

The baby she'd never thought she'd have was already more than a heartbeat, already more than a dream. In a shocked daze she'd barely heard the specialist promise to send her a video of the scan. She didn't recall heading down to the ER, clutching her prenatal prescription, to arrange a couple of weeks off before getting into her car and driving with no real destination in mind.

She'd found herself at the Horseshoe Bay ferry terminal and had purchased a ticket to Vancouver Island before she'd even known that she was heading home.

Pressing a shaky hand to her belly, where a miracle bloomed, where life blazed defiantly despite the odds, Dani wondered how her parents would react to the news that their divorced daughter was pregnant. How they would feel about her bringing up her child alone.

They loved her and would support her no matter what—she knew that. It wasn't like a hundred years ago, or even fifty, when women had been ostracized for having children out of wedlock. She'd be fine. *They'd* be fine. Lots of women brought up children alone and they turned out great. It wasn't as if she *needed* a man. She didn't. She had a great support system who would only be too happy to help.

The last thing she wanted was a man around just for the sake of his child. Not that she would keep the child from Dylan, Dani mused but that kind of relationship was doomed to fail from the start. Considering her one and only attempt at marriage had been such a disaster, there was no way she'd attempt another.

Besides, Dylan didn't love her. How could he? They'd only known each other a short time—although it seemed much longer. He liked the sex they were having but he didn't love her and probably never would. What they had was explosive chemistry, and even explosions eventually lost energy and petered out.

Would he think she'd lied? *Probably.* Would he think she'd deliberately tried to trap him? *Definitely.*

Oh God, she thought with a shudder, he was going to be furious. He'd demand she get rid of it and then he'd make sure she lost her job, and—

No, she chastised herself. That was Richard—not Dylan. But that didn't mean he'd want to be tied to her because of an unplanned pregnancy. She knew how he felt about that. About that woman in West Africa.

It might be the worst possible time to discover that her scarring had healed but she couldn't—*wouldn't*—be sorry. Not when she so desperately wanted this baby. *Her* baby.

A little thrill worked its way past the panic. Her little miracle. Hers and Dylan's.

Dylan. Panic replaced the thrill until her chest ached and her vision swam. What would she say? What *could* she say?

Oh, by the way, remember I told you I have Asherman's? Well…funny story…seems like the doctor was wrong. And not only was he wrong but I guess he miscalculated the possibility of me falling pregnant too. So how do you feel about being called Daddy?

Sure—she could just imagine how well *that* would go down.

Not.

He deserved to know—he *was* going to be a father, after all—but not yet. Not until she'd had time to get used to the idea herself—time to accept that a miracle had touched her life. And time, she thought fatalistically, to brace herself for the fallout.

For the seventh time in less than two minutes Dylan checked the address Maddie had given him and tried to ignore the annoying GPS voice telling him he'd reached his destination.

That was really great, he thought dryly as he studied the neat house overlooking the Georgia Strait, where Dani had supposedly grown up. But what it *didn't* tell him was why she'd come here when her life and her job were in Vancouver.

He'd had no idea that she'd even been *thinking* of leaving the city. Leaving *him*. Early Wednesday morning, when he'd gone to the ER in search of her, he'd been missing her and planning a romantic weekend away. He'd found her curled up on the sofa in the break room and something powerful had moved through him as he'd dropped to his haunches and smoothed the messy curls off her face.

He'd kissed her soft sleepy mouth, his body tightening when she'd hummed in the back of her throat and slid languid fingers through his hair. He'd left her looking flushed and aroused, as though she'd been missing him too.

By the next day she was gone.

For almost forty-eight hours she hadn't answered her phone or returned any text messages. He'd been frantic, thinking something bad had happened to her, and had called every hospital in the city to find out if she'd had an accident and wasn't able to call him. For God's sake, she'd been dizzy and nauseous for weeks—she could have passed out behind the wheel of her car.

When he'd finally heard from her it had been a hurried voice message saying that something had come up and she'd be out of town for a while.

That had been a week ago—which was how long it had taken him to clear his schedule and, more importantly, track her down.

The ball of slow-burning anger that had lodged in his chest right beside fear and concern flared brighter. She'd kissed him as though she couldn't get enough—as though he was more to her than a colleague and neighbor with benefits—and then she'd just walked away.

He hadn't heard anything from her since that cryptic message five days ago that had made his gut clench with fear and his chest tighten.

"Hi, it's Dani," she'd said, sounding shaky. "I'm... Uh... Something came up and I'll be out of town...a while." She'd paused and exhaled noisily before continuing. "Look, Dylan, I... we..." She'd cleared her throat. *"Oh boy,"* she'd muttered. "This is hard. There's just a few... um...*things* I need to take care of. I'll... I'll call you, okay? Soon...later. Um...bye."

It was obvious even to a blind man that she was either in some kind of trouble or she was dumping him. And if she was in trouble why hadn't she come to him? Surely she knew he'd be there for her? Surely she had to know that he was falling for her?

Hell, he'd done everything but give her the words.

Was that why she'd run? Why she wasn't answering or returning his calls? Had she realized that he'd ignored their "temporary" rule and started thinking long-term? Had she panicked because she wasn't feeling the same?

Neither her friends in the ER nor Maddie knew anything—or if they did they weren't talking.

When he'd called Cole's sister to find out if she knew where Dani had gone, and why, the first words out of her mouth had been, "What have you done?"

Maybe he was a clueless male but he had absolutely no idea. And if he listened to her voice message over and over—more to hear her voice than to figure out what she *wasn't* saying—no one had to know but him.

Her disappearance had hit him hard, left him reeling. He'd sat on his empty houseboat feeling as though someone had ripped open his chest and stuck a jagged stake through his heart. Unable to stand his bed without her in it, he'd crashed on the sofa, only to stare at the roof all night.

It was during those dark hours that he'd finally admitted the sobering truth. He wasn't falling for Dani. He'd already fallen—with a rude jolt. And, lying there, all he'd been able to think about was how bleak the future would be without her in it.

He was crazy in love—the can't eat, can't sleep, can't think kind of insanity—with a woman who gave *covert ops* a bad name. Hell, special forces could learn a thing or two about escape-andevade tactics from one sweet and frustratingly elusive ER doctor with big gray eyes and a husky laugh.

But, then again, Dylan hadn't become the best reconstruction ortho surgeon in British Columbia by sitting back and letting success come to him. And he'd be damned if he'd meekly wait around for Dani to get around to dumping him in person.

He knew about her marriage and he understood why she was wary of men and commitment. But she hadn't really given them a chance. The entire time they'd been together she'd had one foot out the door, despite all his efforts to lure her all the way in.

Now, clenching his jaw, he shoved open the Jeep's door and slid out, slamming it behind him, ignoring the fear edging his frustration. He *had* to get her back, he admitted to himself. Life just wasn't the same without her.

Looking forward to the coming confrontation, he started down the driveway to the house and took the steps in a single bound. Dani's battered sedan was the only car out front, so he was confident he had the right address. But after five minutes of punching the doorbell he was still outside, cooling his jets.

After a brief battle with himself he set off around the house, beginning to panic because she might be lying injured somewhere. Maybe she was still dizzy and had fallen and hit her head. Maybe she was bleeding out and needed an ambulance. Maybe… Yeah, he thought with a disgusted snort. And maybe he needed to get a damn grip.

She could be out shopping or… Or out with another man, he thought darkly. Maybe this wasn't her parents' house but the home of an old lover—or maybe a new lover. Maybe she'd met someone else and didn't know how to tell him.

Battling his visions of her lying helpless and unconscious—or laughing with another man—he headed around the house, passing flowerbeds in a profusion of colors and a neat vegetable garden that looked well-tended, reaching a sprawling deck overlooking the strait. Although it was obvious by the empty glass and abandoned book that someone had recently been sitting there, it was now deserted. The sliding doors were locked and the house appeared empty.

He was just about to return to his car and wait

for someone to show up when he noticed an open gate at the end of the landscaped garden. Realizing it opened onto some steps that led to the beach, he followed his instincts and found himself on a sweep of forest-ringed sand littered with rocks, driftwood and beach debris.

A visual sweep told him it was deserted, except for a single figure about a quarter-mile away. He knew instinctively that it was Dani, sitting hunched on the sand while a dog played in the nearby surf, barking at the seagulls and chasing the crabs.

At the sight of her something in his chest expanded and squeezed with a painful clench. Anger flared, and even if it hid an all-encompassing relief that she was okay he wasn't about to let it distract him from his purpose. He was going to get answers and he was done with playing her games.

Flexing his jaw, Dylan took off down the beach toward the only person in the world who could make him crazy. The one woman, he'd realized this past week, he could not—*would* not—live without. She'd sneaked past his defenses, burrowed under his skin and dug deep furrows into his soul, filling them with her sweetness, her surprisingly wicked sense of humor and with the quiet gray eyes that could look into him and see everything.

She'd teased him with something he never thought he'd find.

A future.

Now all he needed was to get her to accept that he could be *her* future too.

CHAPTER ELEVEN

WHEN THE TONE of Polo's bark changed, Dani turned to see what had disturbed him and froze at the sight of the figure walking along the beach toward her.

No, she amended, her heart fluttering with both excitement and apprehension. *Stalking* toward her. Like a large hungry predator with his unsuspecting prey in sight.

Dylan.

Hands jammed deep in his jeans pockets, he radiated a kind of masculine intent that sent exhilaration shooting up her spine along with a healthy dose of wariness. It was there in the set of his wide shoulders, in the deceptively lazy movement of his long muscular legs, and it was all she could do not to bolt to her feet and take off in the opposite direction.

Oh God, she thought, her belly cramping with nerves. He'd found her before she was ready.

Found her before she could shore up her shaky defenses.

With determination in every line of his big, tough body he closed the distance and she knew there was no escaping what was to come. No escaping *him*.

But then again, she thought, swallowing past the lump of emotion forming in her throat, maybe she'd never really had a chance. Maybe her fate had been sealed the moment they'd met—the moment she'd looked up into those moss-green eyes and heard him ask if she was okay.

She wasn't okay. She'd *never* be okay again. And waiting for him to cross those last hundred yards left her jittery and excited.

This is it, she thought as resignation filled her. *Time's just run out*.

And yet she couldn't stop her gaze from clinging, filing away the image of him as he came toward her, so big and safe and familiar. Familiar and yet there was something new…something just a little bit dangerous in the way he'd locked onto her like a heat-seeking missile.

His mouth and his shadowed jaw were set in grim lines, exaggerated by the dark aviator wraparounds that hid his eyes from view. He looked both familiar and foreign. It was that foreignness that had Dani inhaling shakily and drawing her knees to her chest.

Wrapping her arms around her shins, she waited.

Sensing her distress, Polo trotted over, whining and pressing his body against hers. Glad of his comforting presence, she slung an arm around him and hugged him close as Dylan came up behind her.

For long moments he said nothing. The air seemed to prickle with awareness, and the heavy silence frayed her already ragged nerves.

Finally, he said quietly, "You're a difficult woman to find."

There was no sign in his deep voice of the tension she could feel blasting off him in waves.

Feeling unbearably drained—inexplicably miserable—she dropped her forehead to her knees. "What are you doing here, Dylan?"

"The bigger question," he drawled roughly, "is what are *you* doing here, when your life, your job, your *friends* are in Vancouver?" He didn't have to say that *he* was in Vancouver but it hung in the air between them like an unspoken challenge.

Feeling at a disadvantage, she sighed and rose

to her feet, staggering when the abrupt change in elevation had her blood pressure plummeting.

He cursed and snatched her against him before she could face-plant in the sand at his feet. "You're still sick? Have you seen a physician?"

The urge to cling was too great to ignore and she found herself clutching his shirt, her body taking advantage of his heat and strength. She felt weak as a kitten, so tempted to just lay her head against his chest and close her eyes.

She shook her head to clear it. God, she was so tired. She just wanted to slide into sleep but she needed all her wits about her.

"You haven't?" he demanded softly, his long surgeon's fingers digging into the flesh of her upper arms as though he was fighting a battle within himself as to whether he would shake her or pull her close. "This has gone on long enough."

She heard him through the roar of blood in her ears and could only shake her head.

"Let me take you back. I'll examine you myself."

Her throat unlocked enough for her to croak, "No." She shoved at him and stood swaying for a moment while her head cleared. "You won't."

She made herself move away when all she

wanted to do was sink into him and take a nap. But she couldn't—didn't have the right. Not with what she was keeping from him.

"I'm fine."

"You're clearly not," he countered, frustration and concern making him scowl at her. "Not when just rising to your feet leaves you shaky and pale."

He cursed when she blew out a gusty breath.

"Fine," he said curtly, pulling out his phone. "I'm calling an ambulance. Once you're at a hospital I'll order a batch of tests and find out what's wrong."

Shoving her tangled hair off her face, she gave a laugh as shaky as her legs. "That's ridiculous."

She sighed and rubbed her face, hoping to get some feeling back into her numb cheeks while he just narrowed his eyes.

"I don't need an ambulance. I just need a week, that's all. *A week*. I told you I need to sort out some…uh…stuff." She pressed her fingers against her pounding temples and wished they wouldn't throb in counterpoint to her racing pulse. "Go home, Dylan. *Please*. I'm fine. It's nothing a week being fussed over by my mother won't cure."

Nothing seven months won't cure, a voice in her head reminded her.

"And then I'll be back. I promise."

"You've had a week," he pointed out curtly, studying her with narrow-eyed intensity. "And I'm here because you haven't told me *anything*. How can you when you won't answer my damn texts or return my calls."

"I did call. I left a message."

"That garbled confusion? It told me *nothing*, Dani, and it scared me more than if you'd just told me to get lost."

"Is…is that what you thought?" Noisily, she expelled the breath she was holding. Bending, she scratched Polo's ear—to soothe herself as much as the dog. Voice low, she said, "That's not what this is about."

His sigh had her straightening, facing him warily.

"Then why don't you tell me what it *is* about?"

She opened her mouth to tell him but chickened out. "I'm…uh…how did you find me?"

One dark eyebrow rose mockingly up his forehead.

She sighed. "Maddie."

"Don't blame Maddie," he said roughly. "She's

worried about you—*everyone's* worried about you. Besides, I shouldn't have had to hear about it from someone else."

She froze. *It?*

His words sent a shudder of panic through her, because it appeared her nightmare was coming true. He…he *knew*? Knew and was furious?

Of course he'd be furious, she chided herself. After another woman had tried to trap him with an unplanned pregnancy how did she *think* he'd feel?

Heart pounding, she searched his expression for any hint of knowledge that she was pregnant but his face was unreadable, giving nothing away. For a moment she wished he'd remove his sunglasses but she was terrified of what she'd see if he did.

But…*how* could he know? She hadn't told *anyone*. Not even her boss. The only reason Amy knew was because she'd insisted on Dani taking the test and seen her after the gyno appointment had confirmed it.

She felt her face drain of color and locked her shaking knees. "She t-told you?" she asked faintly, ignoring the odd searching look he sent her.

"Of course she told me. She's worried—*I'm*

worried." He folded his arms across his chest. "Didn't you think I'd want to know?" he demanded. "Didn't you think I *deserved* to know?"

Her eyes widened. Panicked, she swallowed and took a hasty step backward, murmuring an absent apology when she bumped into Polo. "I… uh—"

He interrupted her with a rough laugh and spun away to thrust impatient hands through his tousled hair. "Yeah, I can see it didn't even cross your mind."

The muscle jumping in his tight jaw drew Dani's fascinated gaze.

"For God's sake, Dani," he rasped. "What the *hell's* the matter with you?"

Rattled, filled with guilt, she burst out with, "I'm s-sorry. I didn't know, Dylan, I *swear*. I thought…"

Tears pricked her eyes and she blinked rapidly before they could fall and complete her humiliation.

"I thought—" She bit her lip and wrapped her arms around herself in an effort to keep from falling apart. "I thought I c-couldn't, you know… Well, the doctor said it was impossible… I just took his word for it and…well, after that first time we…you… Well, we didn't. And…and then Amy insisted… And it was p-positive…which I didn't believe…"

She was aware she was babbling incoherently but she couldn't seem to stop. Her teeth had begun to chatter and she'd balled her hands into fists beneath her armpits.

"Because it was im-impossible, right?" She broke off to suck in a couple of shallow breaths, knowing she was hyperventilating. "B-besides, you *know* those th-things aren't always reliable. Well, anyway, I made an…an appointment and… I'm sorry."

Her voice cracked and she struggled for a moment to regain control of it.

"I didn't tell you, Dylan, and I'm sorry. But I… I couldn't… I just *couldn't*. I know you're angry but—"

The sob she'd been holding in burst out before she could push it back. Spinning away, she pressed the heels of her hands to her burning eyes. The last thing she wanted was for him to see her fall apart like this.

"You're angry, and I don't blame you… *God*, I'm sorry. But I *couldn't*—" Overcome, she covered her face with her hands and struggled to get her emotions under control. "I couldn't tell you," she said, hoping she could make him understand. "I was in shock and I just… I just had to get away."

For the next few moments the only sounds were her ragged breathing and the gentle shushing of the water as it ebbed and flowed against the sand. How could it be so peaceful when her life was falling apart?

Finally, she could stand the silence no longer. Shoving her hair off her hot face, she chanced a glance over her shoulder and saw that he was staring at her as though she'd babbled state secrets in a foreign language.

"What the *hell* are you talking about?"

He sounded so baffled that for a moment she could only stare at him, wondering if she'd crash-landed in an alternate universe. *Okay*, she thought, so maybe he *doesn't* know. Maybe he's talking about something else…

Licking her lips, she shifted her feet, nervously brushing at the sand clinging to her jeans. "What…what do you…um…*think* I'm talking about?" she asked casually.

For about five seconds he stared at her silently, before abruptly shaking his head as if to clear it.

"Oh, no," he muttered, yanking his sunglasses off and tossing them onto the sand. "No more evasions, dammit. No more evasions and no more lies. Just tell me the *truth.*"

Her heart jolted in her chest as her spine snapped straight. "I never lied to you."

She'd kept things from him maybe, but she'd never lied.

His turbulent green eyes were laser-sharp and she wished for just an instant that they were still hidden behind those dark frames. They made her a little nervous, because he seemed to see right into her soul, to root out all her secrets, all her irrational fears and all her tentative dreams.

"Maybe not," he conceded slowly, "but you haven't been honest with me either. You've kept parts of yourself locked away. You've shared your body but not your mind—and certainly not your emotions."

Her denial was swift and heated. "That's not true. I—"

"*Isn't* it?" he interrupted smoothly. "Isn't that what you're doing right now? Isn't that what you've been doing the past ten days by disappearing without a word? By not returning my calls?"

Dani opened her mouth to hotly deny it, then snapped it shut. What could she say? He was right. She *hadn't* shared herself with him when he'd been generous to a fault.

Blinking rapidly at the realization that she'd selfishly held herself back, Dani could only manage, "I—"

"What do I have to do to prove I'm not like your ex?"

Furious with herself—with him—Dani snapped out, "I never said you were!"

Realizing she was all but shouting, she inhaled to steady herself before lowering her voice.

"I never *thought* you were, Dylan. Not once."

"Maybe," he agreed wearily. "But you can't deny you've been waiting for an opportunity to bolt, Dani. Waiting for me to turn into a lying, cheating bastard."

The truth of it burned a path down her throat. "I'm not. I *haven't*—"

"Haven't you?" he challenged tiredly. "You think I don't see it in your eyes sometimes? Like right now? For just an instant you freeze, and it's like you're bracing yourself for me to turn into some kind of monster who slaps women around."

"I don't think that, Dylan," she assured him,

her voice low, intense. "If I'm waiting…" She swallowed convulsively. "If I've *been* waiting, it's for you to get tired of me."

He blinked in surprise. "Tired? What do you mean, tired?"

"As in lose interest in me," she snapped, rubbing her hands down her arms to ward off a chill that had nothing to do with the breeze that had kicked up. "Get bored. Move on. D-dump me."

He stared at her as though she'd lost her mind, which she very likely had.

"Dump you? You think I'm *dumping* you?"

He shook his head as though he couldn't believe what he was hearing. When she said nothing he inhaled, as if searching for patience.

"What is this really about, Dani? And don't give me that garbage about waiting for me to get bored. If anything, I've been thinking—" He broke off. "Yeah, well, clearly I've been an idiot."

"Dylan…?"

Ignoring her soft, hesitant query, he asked, "Did I really give you the impression that I was getting bored?"

When she said nothing, he sighed and scrubbed his hands over his face, as he sometimes did when he was frustrated. *"Oh."* He gave a rusty laugh. "I get it. Guess I'm a little slow on the uptake, huh? Because I have to tell you I didn't see this coming."

"What—?"

"Is *that* what this is about?" he asked. "You're telling me that *you're* bored? With us? With me?"

She couldn't prevent her shocked denial from emerging any more than he could prevent his shoulders hunching and another ragged laugh bursting out.

"Okay." He sucked in air, let it out again. "Okay…" he said again, dropping his hands on her shoulders and tugging her closer. "So if you haven't found someone else, and you aren't dumping me…what's really the problem?"

Tears filled her eyes and she dropped her forehead wearily against his chest, loving the scent of him, the heat of his body that seeped into hers. Inhaling it because it might be her last opportunity to do so.

She bit her lip and rolled her forehead in denial. If only she could just sink against him and let him take care of everything. She was so tired. Tired of being alone, of being strong and handling stuff alone because she didn't want to worry the people who loved her.

Swallowing a sob, she pressed her face into his warm throat. "It…it wasn't on purpose, Dylan," she murmured tightly. "You have to believe me."

He rubbed a couple of circles on her shoulders before wrapping his hand around her neck and nudging her chin up with his thumb. "*What*, babe?" he asked gently. "What wasn't on purpose?"

Because she couldn't bear to see those beautiful green eyes turn hard as emeralds she dropped her gaze to the soft cotton stretched across his heated flesh and absently realized that her fingers were wrapped tightly in the warm fabric, clinging.

Consciously relaxing, she smoothed out the wrinkles. His deep voice rumbled beneath her palms.

"Dani?"

Before she could chicken out she took a deep breath and got it out quickly, breathlessly. "I'm pregnant."

For a couple dozen heartbeats there was absolutely no reaction except for a reflexive tightening of his fingers. Then he sucked in a harsh breath and, because she couldn't stand not knowing, she quickly looked into his face. Then promptly wished she hadn't.

Oh boy. He looked as though she'd punched him in the head.

Okay, not exactly the reaction she'd hoped to see but better than anger, right? Frazzled by his speechless shock, she shoved away from him and before he could recover filled the silence.

"Don't worry," she assured him quickly. "This is my problem and I'll deal with it. There's no need for you to concern yourself. I'll… I'll handle everything. We'll be fine."

When she paused to suck in a frantic breath, Dylan lifted a hand to silence her. "Hold on," he ordered hoarsely. "Just hold the damn *on*. You're not ill? You haven't been diagnosed with cancer or…or something else?" He shook his head. "You're…*pregnant*?"

"I…uh…yes," she said baldly. "I'm p-pregnant."

The hands he shoved through his hair shook. "You're pregnant and you let me think you were…?" He broke off, swore. "You let me think you were ill and didn't want to tell me?"

She was shocked at the harsh emotion in his voice. "I did not… I wouldn't! I'm not sick!"

He swore again. "Do you have *any* idea what

I've been going through? Thinking...thinking the worst, when all this time—?"

"I *told* you," she babbled, horrified by what he'd been thinking. "I told you I was f-fine."

"No, you told me 'something came up,'" he snapped, storming away a short distance before rounding on her. "Something came up and you had some *things* to sort out and— *Oh*." He staggered back a couple of steps, his gaze dropping to her still flat belly. His mouth fell open. He lifted dazed eyes. "You're...*pregnant*?"

Her lips pressed together. "Yes. And, before you ask, it's yours."

He sent her a searing look. "Don't insult me. Of course it's mine. But—" His expression darkened with concern. "Are...are you sure? What about the Asherman's? Are you okay? Maybe you should be resting?"

Tears filled her eyes and, misunderstanding, he grabbed her and jerked her into his arms.

"There's something wrong, isn't there?" he demanded shakily. "Please tell me there isn't anything wrong with the baby. With you."

She gave a ragged watery laugh and shook her head. "No," she soothed, unconsciously stroking unsteady fingers over his pounding heart.

"There's nothing wrong. I'm fine and yes, I'm sure."

She sucked in a wobbly breath, letting her tears dampen his throat as her heart beat in rhythm with his.

"I saw the scan. I have a picture. And Nicole Dawson sent me a video. It's...*amazing*." She sniffed inelegantly. "Anyway, she says the scarring must not have been as severe as Dr. Cartwright thought, or maybe I just healed better than expected."

She exhaled shakily before sucking in another breath.

"I'm okay. Still in shock, I think. But I've been resting. And my mother's enjoyed pampering me. Me and the baby, we're both fine...or *will* be the further along we get. As long as I don't overdo things."

"It's settled, then," Dylan said, wrapping her close and pressing his lips to her temple. "After we're married you can cut down on your hours or even stop working until after the baby is born. You can move in with me immediately and—What?"

Dani had stilled and was easing out of his arms. She backed off a couple of steps, more to

268 PREGNANT BY THE PLAYBOY SURGEON

resist temptation than to stop his words. "We're
not getting married, Dylan," she said flatly, rubbing at the pinch in her chest. Pinch? Hell, it was
like a mortal wound that bled at the expression
on his face.

He was staring at her as though she'd pulled
back and slugged him in the mouth. "Of course
we're getting married," he countered. "As soon
as we can arrange it—"

"No, we're not," she interrupted furiously. "I've
been married. I'm already a statistic and I'm not
going there again. Not just because I'm pregnant.
Marriage should be for people who love each
other—like my parents, *your* parents. Besides,"
she continued frantically when his expression
hardened, became blank, as though she'd hurt
him somehow when that was impossible, "this
isn't the nineteenth century. A woman doesn't
have to get married anymore just because she's
pregnant. Don't forget what you told me about
that woman in West Africa. You wouldn't marry
Simone just because she was pregnant."

"Forget Simone," he growled, clearly furious
that she was using his own words against him.
"I wasn't in love with her."

She stilled, her gaze searching. "What are you saying?"

"I'm saying I'm in *love* with you, dammit," he snapped. "I've been in love with you for days… weeks…maybe from the first."

Her eyes widened and she jerked back, a host of expressions tripping over each other as they crossed her face: shock, fear, hurt…denial.

"Yeah, I can see that thrills the hell out of you." He spun away. "Surely you're not surprised?" he demanded. "An intelligent woman like you? How could you not know when it's been there every time I've looked at you? Every time I've touched you, kissed you? Every time we've made love?"

Her throat closed and it felt as if she was trying to push her words through jagged glass shards. "Don't…" she gasped, pressing a tight fist against the pain in her chest. "Don't you *dare* p-pretend something you don't feel just because you think it's…it's what I want to hear. I'm not your responsibility, Dylan. Besides, it's not like I'm expecting anything from you. I told you— I'll handle it myself."

He muttered a few choice curses. "I've just told you I'm in love with you and all you can say is you're not my responsibility? Of *course* you are.

You weren't alone in that bed, Dani and I'll be damned if you shut me out because you're afraid of your emotions. Heck, *look* at you—you're terrified of *mine*."

"Don't—don't do this to me, Dylan, please," she sobbed, swiping angrily at the tears that rolled down her cheeks. "I'm trying to be strong here because I can't… I c-couldn't…stand it if…if we got married and one day you m-met someone more suitable and…and then hated me." She gulped and wrapped her arms protectively around her belly, where their child grew. "Hated *us* for being there, for standing in your way. You'd hate that, Dylan, and you'd hate *me*."

Dylan rocked back on his heels, studying her as though he'd never seen her before. "You really have a low opinion of me, don't you?"

Dani blinked. "What? No!" she denied hotly. "I think the world of you. If I didn't I wouldn't be in l—"

"Wouldn't be what?" he demanded when she stopped abruptly and just stared at him, as though she'd admitted to a deadly sin. "Throwing my feelings in my face?"

"I—"

"Give me a chance, Dani," he urged quietly,

stepping closer to brush a tangled curl off her forehead with gentle fingers. "I've showed you in a thousand ways just how much you suit me... how much we suit each other."

Dani couldn't resist turning her face into his caress, stepping into his big hard body. "I... I'm scared," she admitted in a quiet rush. "I'm scared I'll disappoint you. I couldn't bear that."

Wrapping her close, Dylan dropped his cheek to the dark tangle of wind-tossed curls. "You couldn't," he murmured. "Don't you know by now that the only way you could ever disappoint me is by cutting me out of your life?"

He smoothed a hand down her back, over her hip to her belly, so he could press his palm where his child grew.

"Let me love you—both of you. I know you don't—perhaps can't—feel the same but I love you enough for both of us."

Her body jolted against his. "Dylan...?" she murmured, lifting her head. Huge gray eyes swirled with fierce emotion as they tentatively met his.

"Let's make a future," he urged quietly, dropping a gentle kiss on her soft mouth. "Together."

For a moment her mouth remained passive and he felt his heart sink, quietly break. Then her lips trembled and she gave a ragged moan. Her hand stole to his, pressed it where it lay against her belly.

"You...*love* me?"

"Can't you feel it?" he murmured against her mouth. "Can't you feel it every time I touch you? Every time we're together?"

She pressed closer, her mouth curving against his. "I thought we just had really great chemistry."

He chuckled and pushed her away so he could see her face, no longer pale and unhappy but flushed, glowing, beautiful. "We do. But it's more than that, Dani. It's...*more*."

"I..."

He watched her dark lashes sweep down to cover her gaze. When they lifted, the emotion burning in the silvery depths staggered him.

"I love you, Dylan." She lifted his hand to her face, pressed it against her cheek. "I didn't want to but I couldn't help myself."

"I know," he murmured, his thumb soothing her cheekbone. "I'm irresistible."

She gave a laughing snort and turned, biting

his thumb. "Yeah, lucky for you. Because it's not like you have anything *else* going for you."

He chuckled but soon sobered. "I *am* lucky," he agreed softly, fiercely. "Make me even luckier by setting a date."

And because he was holding her he felt the tremor go through her. Her gaze turned wary and he could feel her pulling away. Even though she hadn't moved.

"Date?"

"Our wedding—"

She quickly slid one slender finger over his lips before replacing it with her mouth. "Not now," she murmured against his lips. "Ask me again. If you still want to get ma—" She stopped and cleared her throat. She huffed out a shaky laugh. "If you still want to do…um…*that* by the time our baby is born, ask me again then."

"Wow," he said, amused. "You can't even *say* it, can you?"

"Of course I can," she spluttered, going red. "It's just…it's such a big step, Dylan, a huge… *thing*. I don't want to mess up again."

"You won't," he said, with a conviction she didn't seem to share. "But, hypothetically speaking," he added casually, "if I asked you again, when our baby is born, you'd say yes?"

Her arms slipped around him, and with her face pressed into his neck she hugged him hard. "Yes," she murmured. "I might just say yes."

Knowing he'd pushed her as far as he could for now, Dylan snatched her off her feet and cupped the back of her head. Pressing a kiss to her laughing mouth, he knew he'd won the war.

EPILOGUE

Six months later

"GOOD JOB, PEOPLE!" Dylan called out, pulling off his mask and cap with one hand while stripping off his gown with the other. Surgery had gone overtime and he was eager to head down to the ER to see how Dani was doing.

She'd been a little pale and tired this morning but had insisted that she was fine. *Soon*, he thought, tossing the soiled garments in the laundry bin and heading for the basins to wash up. Soon he'd insist on her taking maternity leave and he wasn't taking no for an answer.

The past six months had been the happiest of his life, he mused, reaching for the soap and nudging the tap open with his elbow. And even though he hadn't yet managed to tempt her down the aisle he'd made it a habit to sneak a proposal in regularly. Like when she was soft and drowsy and sated, her barriers down.

Just this morning he'd kissed her soft mouth and gently rubbed her growing belly, chuckling when the baby moved beneath his hand. Dani's lips had smiled against his and she'd snuggled closer, making his heart clench with love.

"Soon," she'd murmured, smoothing her hand down over his chest, when he'd asked her again when she'd make an honest man of him. With a contented sigh, she'd pressed her lips to his left pec—right over his heart—and told him she loved him.

Full of her, he'd let it go, even though he wanted to tie her to him so tightly that she'd never get away. Never *want* to get away.

But his mother had warned him to be patient, so he'd be patient.

Even if it killed him.

He was grabbing a handful of paper towels when the outer door slammed open and a nurse burst in, red-faced and out of breath. It looked as if she'd been running. "Dr. St. James?" she demanded, her gaze frantically racing over the remaining surgical staff milling around. "*Where's Dr. St. James?* We've been trying to get hold of h—"

"Here," he interrupted, even as her gaze zeroed in on him. "What's wrong?"

"It's Dani," the woman gasped. "The baby's coming. You have to come quickly."

He was at her side in an instant. "What? It's too soon. Tell me what happened."

"No time," she yelped, shoving him toward the outer doors. "Obstetrics Wing—surgery. They've called Dr. Dawson. *Hurry.*"

Dylan didn't recall tearing through the hospital to the East Wing. Nor did he remember taking the three flights of stairs at a dead run. He was a doctor, *dammit*, a surgeon. He'd been trained to maintain a level head in a crisis. But panic ripped at him as he hit the obstetrics wing and tore through the swing doors with his lungs burning.

Just as he shoved his way into the room he heard a thin wail break through the silence.

Nicole Dawson looked up. "Congratulations, Dad, it's a girl!"

Dani floated lazily up through layers of sleep to hear the steady beeping of machines. It was a familiar sound that comforted her and for a moment—just a split second—she thought she was back on surgical rotation.

Then she remembered seeing the flashing lights, feeling the jostle of the gurney racing down brightly lit passages. And then Dylan's face, his eyes dark and filled with love and concern. She remembered telling him she loved him and then... Nothing.

Her eyes flew open as she tried to heave her body upright. *"Dylan—?"* It was a gasp on her lips, emerging as a kind of gurgling rasp.

She was barely aware of a groggy, "Wha—?" cutting through her panic. But it brought her head around as a disheveled Dylan lurched up from the chair beside the bed, his frantic gaze sweeping the room.

On their return sweep his eyes locked with hers. "What's wrong?" he rasped, his eyes suddenly wide awake and intense. "Are you in pain? Can I get you anything?"

Dani stared at him, vaguely aware of the sound of approaching footsteps.

A young nurse skidded into the doorway, her eyes wide in her pale face. "Is...is everything all right, Dr. St. James?" she demanded.

Clearly realizing that he'd been almost shouting, Dylan cleared his throat. "Everything's fine, thank you," he said quickly.

"Dr. Stevens?" the nurse asked quietly, moving into the room to check the IV cannulas.

"I'd like some iced water, please," Dani said, wanting to buy them some privacy. She waited until the nurse had left before meeting Dylan's gaze. "What's going on?"

He collapsed back into the chair. He looked exhausted. His jaw was rough and dark, his eyes deep pools of some fierce emotion that stole her breath. She couldn't remember ever seeing him look so rattled.

"How are you feeling?" he asked.

"Tired."

His laugh emerged roughly before he leveled a crooked smile at her and reached for her hand, sliding their palms together, lacing their fingers. His were warm and solid, familiar.

Lifting her cold hand, he pressed a kiss to her knuckles. "You couldn't wait, could you?" His fingers tightened around hers. "I sprinted all the way from the West Wing to get here, just in time for Nicole to congratulate me."

She licked dry lips. "What happened? I remember sudden cramps," she admitted. "And then you... Wait... You were holding—"

"Yeah, our daughter," he said, with such pride that Dani blinked. He kissed her knuckles, his eyes warm with love as they clung to hers. "She's beautiful—just like her mother."

A little thrill moved through her. "Where is she?" she demanded urgently, struggling to sit up. "I want to meet her."

"In a minute," he soothed as the nurse hurried in with a glass of iced water. "Let's get you some water first. You have a lot of fluid to replace." He gave the nurse a brief glance as he took the glass in his free hand. "You can bring our daughter now," he said.

"Of course, Dr. St. James."

Watching the departing nurse, Dani gripped his hand. "She's...okay?"

His grin was a white flash in the dim room. "She's better than okay," he said with satisfaction, and dropped a quick kiss on her mouth.

It was a kiss that instantly gentled, clung and after a long sweet moment ended on a sigh. Hers *and* his.

His forehead touched hers. "She's a fighter—

like her mom," he murmured, moving back a couple of inches to look into her eyes.

His gaze, soft and endlessly green, had something tight inside her melting, unfurling.

"She came into the world shaking her fists and bellowing!"

He straightened as the nurse reappeared, pushing a neonatal bassinet into the room.

"Thank you, Nurse Richards, I can take it from here."

Dani's eyes remained locked on Dylan as he gently scooped up the tiny bundle in his big, capable hands.

"Hey, sweetheart," he crooned softly, drawing a sigh from the nurse, who was now checking Dani's vitals. "You're awake. Can't wait to meet your mom, can you?"

He dropped a tender kiss on the infant's forehead, giving Dani a quick glimpse of huge dark eyes, a wealth of dark hair fluffed around a delicate pink face and a tiny rosebud mouth.

"Well, she can't wait to meet *you*." He lifted the swaddled infant as though they shared a secret. "You won't tell her about you know what, will you? She doesn't need to know your dad completely embarrassed himself back there. She doesn't need to know he went a little crazy."

The nurse gave a short chuckle.

Dani arched a brow at him. "If he knows what's good for him," she announced primly, "he'll stop talking and let me meet you."

Grinning, Dylan gently tucked the pink bundle into her arms and pressed a kiss to her temple. But she could only stare down in amazement at her baby.

Their daughter.

Their miracle.

She looked into the perfect little face for the first time—into those slate-gray eyes that looked far too large and wise for such a tiny face—and felt tears spring into her own.

"Oh…" Her breath caught on a huge ball of emotion, because it was like holding a price-less gift—one she'd never expected to receive. "L-look at her, Dylan. She's so perfect and tiny."

Just then the infant opened that delicate rose-bud mouth and yawned, making Dani laugh and cry as love burst through her like a shaft of golden light through heavy cloud.

With her free hand she brushed tender fingers

across a delicate pink cheek and the little face turned toward the touch, rooting hungrily.

Dylan laced his fingers with hers and eased down behind her on the bed, cradling them both—Dani *and* their daughter—against his chest.

Snuggling in, she realized her heart was filled with a fierce kind of joy—joy and gratitude and a new hope for the future.

"She's wonderful, Dylan." She tilted her head back, her eyes meeting his, filled with the staggering thrill of the miracle they had made together and the life that loomed ahead. "And so are you."

Lifting her mouth, she accepted his slow, gentle kiss. A kiss that stirred as it soothed so that even when he slowly ended it her lips clung, not ready—not *nearly* ready—to let go.

It was in that moment she realized with blinding clarity that she didn't have to let go—didn't ever have to. Because she loved him enough to take a chance.

"I don't know what we'd do without you," she murmured, her throat tight with the terrifying emotion that had banished all her fears and uncertainty in one blinding instant.

"It's a good thing you didn't see me last night, then." His chuckle was a deep and wonderful sound. "You might rethink the whole 'wonderful' thing. You might change your mind about making us a family."

She shook her head. "No," she said firmly. "Sophie deserves two people who love her."

For a moment she felt him tense but he must have seen something in her eyes because his gaze turned intense, searching. "And *do* you?" he asked quietly.

Distracted by the overwhelming feelings filling her for this man—this amazingly tender and wonderful man—who'd come to her rescue one rainy night, Dani blinked. "Do I what?"

"Love me?"

Her breath escaped on a soundless sigh because she'd never been more sure of anything. "You know I do."

His hand brushed over the wild fluff of dark hair covering the tiny head of their daughter. "Then say yes," he urged. "Say you'll marry me and make us a family."

With fierce joy bursting through her, Dani turned and smiled up at him. "We're already a family," she murmured, and slid the fingers of her free hand into his hair. She pulled him closer, held him where she knew he belonged. "But, yes," she murmured. "I'll marry you."

And with a softly muttered, "Finally…" Dylan laughed and kissed his future.

* * * * *

LET'S TALK
Romance

For exclusive extracts, competitions
and special offers, find us online:

f facebook.com/millsandboon

⊡ @millsandboonuk

🐦 @millsandboon

Or get in touch on 0844 844 1351*

For all the latest titles coming soon,
visit millsandboon.co.uk/nextmonth

*Calls cost 7p per minute plus your phone company's price per
minute access charge

Want even more
ROMANCE?

Join our bookclub today!

'Mills & Boon books, the perfect way to escape for an hour or so.'

Miss W. Dyer

'Excellent service, promptly delivered and very good subscription choices.'

Miss A. Pearson

'You get fantastic special offers and the chance to get books before they hit the shops'

Mrs V. Hall

Visit millsandbook.co.uk/Bookclub and save on brand new books.

MILLS & BOON